hidden

Forged by Magic, Book 1

M.P. Starkweather

PHOENIX ECLIPSE PUBLISHING

Contents

I want to dedicate this book to my two biggest fans, my husband Josh and my son Thom, who will probably never read any of my books. Thanks for pushing me to chase my dream. I love you both to the moon and back.

Acknowledgments

I would like to thank:

My author besties, who encourage me to keep writing, even when it's hard;

My amazing PA, Gwen, who is my twinsie;

My Alpha Team who tries hard to keep me on track;

My Editing Team who does their best to make sure my books make sense and have as few typos as possible;

My Cover Artist, Ravin DeMarco, who's responsible for the gorgeous images on the front of this book

and My ARC Team, who catch some of the things the rest of us miss.

one

Zoey

Looking back on it now, I should have known to leave that book buried in the library's vault. I should have turned and run in the other direction, but I just couldn't. There was something about it that all but screamed my name. It was begging to be read. The soft amber glow of the pages was irresistible. The hand-stitched leather binding seemed to hum every time I came near it. I'm not sure how no one else even noticed it. It almost seemed as though the book itself was alive and yearned for attention.

As soon as I touched it, I could feel the energy oozing off it. The leather-bound book vibrated with power. My heart raced as I carried it from the vault to my office. I turned it over in my hands several times, inspecting every inch of the fine handiwork. It was dark brown, aged leather with runic symbols on the front and back covers. It seemed most likely to be a journal of sorts, being only five inches wide by seven inches long and four inches thick. I hadn't been able to find time to flip through it, but every day it called to me more and more. It was getting more challenging to complete my daily tasks at the museum, with the book continually tugging at my mind.

The year was 3127. While Earth was still somewhat functional, it was barely habitable, and most people had moved on either to other planets or to the space stations that debuted in 2125. Each space station was divided into specialties, and the inhabitants worked in some particular field. The residents were not all humans, and each station's leadership was based on skill, not the person's race.

The space stations were named after Greek gods and goddesses, based on each station's primary purpose. Calliope 127 housed the museum and library. We just called it Calliope, though. People came from all over the galaxy to visit and tour it. In addition to housing the museum and the library, Calliope had an engineering hub and a tech research wing. There were also shopping zones, a residential section, a hotel wing, and restaurants to accommodate both the inhabitants' and visitors' needs. Each space station was a self-sustained "planet" that had everything needed to survive. The only reason to travel between them was a change in a specialty or just to see something new.

Before they became self-sustaining in the early days of the space stations, everything was shipped up from Earth. There were shuttles carrying deliveries almost every day. They would bring food, clothing, electronics, parts...just about anything you could imagine. The more advanced Calliope became, the less we needed to import from Earth, and the more the planet seemed to fail. People either moved up to Calliope or relocated to other space stations. Some moved to other worlds, but there weren't many compatible with human anatomy, so choices were limited. As the people left, factories and cities became abandoned. Soon the once beautiful planet of Earth was just an empty shell. Not that I knew any of this from experience. I had the right job as the curator of the museum on Calliope to read about it.

Working at the museum had its benefits. Even with the technological advances, there seemed always to be a need for anthropology. When it came to be paired with magic after the gifted won the Great Galactic War in 2109, witchcraft was no longer outlawed. And by magic, I don't mean parlor and card tricks or sleight of hand—I mean "I once saw my neighbor Myrtle turn her husband into a frog because he refused to take the trash out" magic. Don't worry; I'm almost sure she turned him back once he agreed to help with the chores. No one was sure what had caused the rise of magic, but it had happened on a human holiday called Halloween in the 1980s. Of course, there were stories and fairy tales about it, but nothing concrete in the history books explained how it had happened. And wouldn't it figure...the one person who knew the most about magic, me, didn't even have any.

At this point, most people had all but forgotten about printed books. With the newest electronic devices from Amazon, Apple, and Google, who could blame them? But I always loved the feel of an actual paper, bound book. The smell of them called to me like a siren song. My love of books is why I have the perfect career. Being an anthropologist helped me to get the curator position at the space station museum. With the shortage of trees because of industrialization, books are no longer printed and haven't been in centuries, so every book that exists is considered an artifact. Thus, most of the books from Earth belong to the museum and are under my care. Outside of the museum, people had special permits to have printed books, though we never understood why. It seems strange that the Galactic Council would be concerned with them, but I'm sure they had their reasons.

Most existing books are in my care, circling us back to the tome—everything seems to circle back to that thing. It turned out the glowing, leather-bound masterpiece that was hand-crafted was, in fact, a journal, written and bound thousands of years ago. I was utterly unprepared for what I saw when I opened it. Nothing in my life could have made me ready for that.

I ran my hands across the perfect stitching as the book vibrated more fiercely. I had no choice but to open it and see what secrets it held. I pulled the massive book over to me with awe, sat in my chair, and lifted the front cover. The pages glowed brighter for a minute and then stopped. I stared in wonder, my face as blank as the pages in front of me.

"Blank! How can it be blank?" I asked myself. "That's just not possible. Did the ink fade over the years? I'll have to test a page, though I hate to ruin such a beautiful piece." I closed it and opened the cover again.

"Ugh, I just can't. This journal is the weirdest thing. Why am I so drawn to a blank book?" I ran my hand over the clean white page in amazement. Even after thousands of years, it looked brand new. It was the strangest thing—today, the pages looked brand new, but I could have sworn yesterday that they looked aged and yellowed. Then it hit me: this is no ordinary book. It'll take a little magic to tap into her secrets. I pushed my chair back from the desk, stood up, and paced across the floor and back. Maybe the Goddess Calliope would help me since books and creativity were her areas of expertise.

"Goddess Calliope, please help me. I feel drawn to this book; I need to know what it holds. I feel like I'm being called for a reason. I'd like your blessing to read the words within this magical book."

I closed my eyes, reached down, and touched the page. It began to glow once more, and letters appeared. I jumped and pushed the book away as if it were a snake coiled to strike. I was both shocked and curious and more than a little scared. Part of me wanted to throw the book and run as far away as I could. I'm not sure how long I stood there staring at it in terrified silence.

In the end, curiosity won out, and I found myself sitting back down, pulling the book closer, and preparing to read what appeared. The letters seemed to be a strange alien language that I couldn't read. It wasn't clear to me which language it was, either, though I had studied most known languages and was proficient in at least a dozen.

"Are you kidding me? These ridiculous symbols are what I was so obsessed with? I can't even read it! I guess it wasn't meant for me after all."

Suddenly, the words started to change. I eyed the book with disgust and frustration. I wasn't sure how to translate a text that was in an unknown language.

"Great. Now I've made it mad, and it's going to change to a different language or more blank pages. And now I'm talking about the book as if it were a person. I've lost my mind." Yet what was just written in one tongue changed to my own.

"How is this even possible?" Even more startling, the words on the page changed again before I could even read them. It now reads:

Ah, Zenovia, my dear, many things are considered impossible, but as you shall soon see, they are indeed not.

"Wait, is this book talking to me? Did it just answer my question? How is this possible?"

I slammed the book shut and rushed from my office toward my living quarters. I didn't even bother with the lift, running straight past it to the rarely used stairwell. As I ran down the stairs to PH-4, so many questions and thoughts ran through my head. PH-4 was the floor that included my parents' rooms and my own.

First and foremost, how did the book know my given name? I don't think anyone here had ever heard my actual name—everyone has always called me Zoey. It was forbidden in my culture to share one's given name with someone outside of your family unit. In our culture, words held power, and it wasn't considered safe to reveal the sacred ones to anyone outside the family unit. As far as I knew, the only people who knew my given name were my parents, and I hadn't seen them in years. I didn't have any brothers or sisters or any other family that I knew of. It had always just been my parents and myself until they left. When the book was cataloged, it was estimated to be at least 2000 years old. There's no way that book could know who I am if it had been written before I was born, right? About halfway to my quarters, I hesitated, then turned left instead of right. I again passed the lift for the stairs, heading back up this time, two floors above my quarters, to H-1.

As much as I dreaded the idea, I had to talk to Race. He would be able to help me figure out how someone altered the book with electronic properties. It had to be electronic, right? The only other possible explanation was magic, but I didn't have enough experience with that to tell. I was pretty sure that Race also had a special scanner that could detect magic. It was a starting point, anyway. And since Race was the head of the tech department for the space station, he was the only one who could help me. In my head, I argued with myself back and forth about this book having electronic elements versus it being magical. I couldn't decide which would be worse.

Unfortunately, that meant a trip to the Holo and potentially an awkward conversation or two. Race isn't his real name; he's been called that since we were young because it's his passion. One day in history class, they were teaching us about culture. There was a lesson on NASCAR, which was a significant thing on Earth before the gas-powered engine ban. Race was obsessed. I just didn't think I would ever understand the idea of driving around in circles to see who was the fastest. But I guess Race had the same feeling about me spending all my time in the library section of the museum.

I hate the Holo. If I were going to escape to an alternate reality, I wanted to do it in a book. Everyone else loved the Holo. I rounded the corner and stood in front of the oversized gray door. The only thing worse than the Holo was that I would have to ask Race for help, and I knew where that would lead. With one deep breath to steady myself, I scanned my entry badge and walked through the door, leaving behind the quiet, gray hall for a fully packed stadium and the revving of engines.

TWO

Zoey

I WATCHED AS THE antique cars raced around the oval track. They were replicas of the gas-powered monsters that were popular around the year 2000 or so. I barely heard Jack call my name over the roar of engines and spectators. I turned toward the pits, where Race's best friend and "crew chief" would be. He started jogging my way as he called out to get my attention. My face lit up when I saw him.

"Hey, Zoey, didn't know you were coming to watch today," Jack said excitedly. "And Race didn't tell me you two were getting back together, either." He was Race's biggest fan and the Head of Engineering, as well as being the only Garlax I've ever met. They had been best friends for the past twenty years. If you wanted to talk to Race, you went through Jack.

Garlax were, from appearance only, a lizard-humanoid hybrid. In truth, they came from Garla-9, in the southern quadrant of the Delta sector. Their lizard-like appearance was an evolutionary adaptation to the atmosphere of the planet. Jack was as good with a wrench as he was with a warp core. He could take anything apart and put it back together again. Jack could also build you anything you could think of. And yeah, Jack is a nickname too. Garlax names are far too complicated for humans and most other races to pronounce. It was just another way the rest of the universe had adapted to appease humans. At times some species were annoyed by the simplicity of them and considered humans to be inferior. The Garlax were one of those species, except for Jack. It probably helped that humans had raised him on the space station from the age of three. He judged people by their actions and personalities, not their species, which was good. I'm sure he, Race, and I made a funny picture when the three of us used to hang out.

I craned my neck to look him in the face as I answered. "We aren't, and I hadn't planned on coming to watch. I need to borrow Race. Got a situation at the museum." Jack crossed his arms on his broad chest as I spoke. His brow furrowed, and I imagined he was trying to comprehend the fact that things weren't going to go back to the way they used to be; Race and I were not going to be a couple again.

"They're almost done. Three laps to go, and Race is in the lead. If he can hold on to it—he just might win this time." Then he turned his attention back to the race. That was Jack's way of telling me he wouldn't call Race to the pits; I would have to wait until the race was over. No harm in watching—at least it was almost over. It's not as though the book was going anywhere. I watched the cars fly around the track. There were only two of them, but it was so loud. I would have thought there were a dozen. It amazed me that anyone could see this as a sport. But if you believe that humans as a species weren't as advanced as some of us, I guess it makes a little more sense. I had always tried not to judge, but sometimes it wasn't easy, especially in situations like this. As I stood there watching, I lost myself in memories.

By the gods, I miss home. My home planet of Zyterra had been located in the western quadrant of the Omega sector. It was one of the smaller worlds there. Not that I remember much about it, but I had been told that my home planet was as beautiful as the Earth used to be before the second Industrial Revolution that resulted in around 80 percent of the earth being paved. It was tragic how the humans were not willing to prevent most of that destruction. Their galactic war was what destroyed my planet and brought my family to the space station. Sometimes humans could be so selfish. I remember it like it was yesterday, even though it was twenty years ago. I was just a child. As a lone tear made its way down my cheek, I heard that booming voice.

"Zoey! Did you see that? I almost had him that time!" Race almost always set the Holo to let him race a computer program of his idol, even though the NASCAR driver who had been called Junior had been dead for more than a few centuries. Yet, every time, Race lost to him. I wasn't quite sure that Race didn't lose on purpose.

"I saw enough, Race. You always almost get him. And this isn't what you think. I didn't just come to watch. I need a favor."

"Yeah, but this time was different. But wait—you're not here to watch me drive, are you? What's wrong? Tell me." He always had the innate ability to read me like a book. I looked into his almond-shaped eyes, reached up, tousled his chin-length, dark purple hair, and responded.

"Of course, I wanted to watch you...but I also need you to look at something." I was pretty sure he would see through the little white lie, but I was trying to smooth things over before he got the wrong idea.

Before I could get anything else out, Jack chimed in, "She said there's an emergency in the museum." Race raised an eyebrow at Jack as he stepped toward his best friend. Jack towered over him, but Race didn't back down. He proceeded to get in Jack's face. Jack's seven-foot stance made Race's five-foot-eleven seem small.

"Why didn't you call me in?" Race asked Jack. I stepped between them, placing my left hand on Race's chest and my right hand on Jack's chest, pushing them apart, to avoid the ass-chewing I'd seen way too many times before. I hoped it didn't come to blows with me in the middle, but it had happened before.

"Wait, wait, *wait!* I never said EMERGENCY; I said *issue.*" I don't think I'll ever understand why Jack loves to get Race riled up like that. "There's an *issue I need your help with.* It's not an emergency. That's why he didn't call you in." But the grin on Jack's face told me that's what he was doing. He liked to see how much he could get Race going, and occasionally it ended in blows. Which generally went in Jack's favor since he was enormous.

"Well, in that case," Race began, as he slipped an arm around my shoulders, "fill me in. What's going on?" I both loved and hated it when he wrapped his arm around me like that. It was too cozy; it would be too easy to lose myself again.

"There's a book in the library; there's something off about it. I need you to check it out. I'm sure someone has tampered with it to add an electronic component somehow. I need to know who and how. Come on; I'll show you."

As soon as I said my problem was with a book, Jack walked away. I could have sworn he cocked an eyebrow first as though it had piqued his interest. I must have imagined it. He wasn't a fan of the library and usually avoided it altogether if he could. Jack preferred to learn by doing rather than reading. But Race used to come to visit me in the library section of the museum, and he enjoyed books from time to time. I watched Jack walk away as Race steered me toward the door.

There was a time I would have wished to follow Jack instead of walking with Race. At one point, I thought he felt the same, but I knew that even if he did, he'd never act on it. Race was like a brother to Jack. It wouldn't have been worth it to either of us. We both cared deeply for Race, and because of that, we let our chance slip away. I sometimes wondered if Jack remembered our conversation from that night. I never asked if he ever regretted that decision. There were moments when I fought against the need to know his answer.

We were just teenagers. Race had broken his arm and had to have reconstructive surgery to repair it. Jack and I both stayed by his side until the nurse kicked us out of the room. After that, we walked back to our rooms, stopping off at the Holo first. I hadn't decided to hate that place yet. Perhaps this particular night was what caused that reaction from me.

Jack created an outdoor scene to relax, with trees, grass, and the most beautiful sunset. We talked about everything that night—hopes, dreams, my failed relationship with Race, and his inability to let me go. There was a point when we were lying in the grass beside each other, and Jack reached for my hand. We lay there for hours, just talking and holding hands. That conversation was the most exciting and devastating I'd ever had. Jack admitted he'd had feelings for me for years, but because Race was his best friend, he had backed off at Race's first mention of being interested.

In the end, we agreed that it was best for the three of us if we didn't try to pursue anything. We also decided to forget about that conversation and never to tell Race any of it. It was painful sometimes to think what might have been. At the same time, it was better for everyone involved because then we all got to remain friends, just like we had always been. There were moments, though, when those feelings came sneaking back. As difficult as it was, I had to push it aside and focus on the book. I felt like there was something big happening here. Besides, just because Jack and I couldn't be together didn't mean I had to get back with Race. There were plenty of other choices out there. Maybe the book would lead me to one of them.

I turned my attention back to Race, who was still talking about his challenge on the track. I tried to act interested, though I'm sure he knew my heart was elsewhere.

THREE

Jack

As soon as Zoey told Race about the book, I acted disinterested and walked away. I knew if I didn't, I'd end up giving details away that I had no real way to explain. There was no way to tell her about her powers or about the book without revealing how I knew. And doing that would jeopardize the mission. I had to walk away while I could. I didn't need Race asking questions either. I loved him, but I had intel he was working for the wrong side on this one, which is why I was doing everything I could to keep them apart. Meaning I would keep telling her that he says they're getting back together because I know it will make her mad, and she'll push him away more.

Well, it was one reason anyway. I tried not to think about the other reason anymore. We had agreed it was better to leave it alone. It wasn't precisely an agreement—more that I told Zoey that I'd never be comfortable hurting my best friend like that. She understood, and we've gone on like it never happened. This many years later, I still imagined feeling her hand in mine from time to time. Usually, when this happened, I would head to the gym and run it off. Denying myself sometimes led to me pushing myself harder and being in better overall shape. I'd make sure I hit the gym when I finished what I had to do.

I still had a couple of leads to run down while I searched for who Race was following. I had my suspicions but couldn't let that interfere. It did no good to report back if I wasn't sure. Once the Holo was cleared out and secured, I headed to my office. I probably looked paranoid, making sure no one was around, but it was warranted. Once inside, I typed a series of passwords into the door lock, disabling the cameras and the safety overrides so that no one could unlock the door. I needed a few minutes of privacy.

I pulled my handheld computer out of my desk drawer, opened a secure connection, and shot an instant message off.

She found it, and he knows.

I only waited a couple of minutes to get the reply.

Keep us apprised of the situation. No action necessary unless he threatens her. She must accept the quest and be allowed to leave. You must make sure she goes safely without letting her know you're involved.

I had expected that response but needed to confirm my next step.

Do I give her the package or wait?

I knew giving it to her would require a level of explanation that none of us was ready for now, but if that's what the boss told me to do, that's what I would do.

Not yet. He's too close. We need to get her away first. You keep the package safe until the time is right. You'll know when.

I acknowledged the response and broke contact. They could contact me if something came up. I sat alone in my office for a few minutes, looking over blueprints and requisition orders to clear my head. I reminded myself of why I took this mission and why I stayed on Calliope when I could have left. I hated hiding who I was and what I was doing from my friends. I knew it was for the best, though.

I was finished with my engineering responsibilities but stayed a while longer, just staring out the window into the void of space outside. This place had been my home for as long as I could remember; these people were my family. Yet I knew that soon I'd be giving it all up to head to the surface.

I remembered the day I was approached for this mission, for this job. Zoey, Race, and I had just graduated from our formal schooling and prepared to head out for our job training. There were so many people at the ceremony that there was no way for me to know who had slipped the note into my pocket. It was reasonably straightforward: *Meet me in the cargo bay at midnight.* Of course, I did because curiosity won out.

"You? But I don't understand. What's this about?" I asked. The look on my face was rewarded with a teasing laugh.

The familiar voice explained that I would have to help protect Zoey so she could find her destiny. I knew going into this precisely what was at stake. I found out that Race had received an identical note that night but had chosen to ignore it in favor of a party. We were selected because we were considered the two people who loved her the most and the only ones who could be trusted. It didn't look good on him that Race had opted to party instead of taking this meeting. In his defense, neither of us knew what the note was about. And since I didn't think he got one, he most likely didn't know I got one either.

Once I accepted the mission, I was guaranteed the Head Engineer position on Calliope to keep me close to Zoey and the book. That book had been on Calliope for years before Zoey found it, or it found her as the case may be. My benefactor handed me a bag of supplies and untraceable credits to cover any expenses related to what they wanted me to do. Among the collections was a box about the size of Zoey's hand. It was wrapped in brown paper and sealed so that any attempt at tampering with it would be apparent. I was taught how to take precautions to ensure privacy in communications, tech skills, and spy skills. The training ran concurrently with my engineering studies, so I wasn't gone any longer than the others, and they had no idea I'd done anything besides continuing my engineering studies. I had to keep everything a secret, and I hated it. I was so tired of hiding my feelings, my thoughts, my actions. But I knew it was for the best. Or at least I hoped it was.

I just had to focus on the mission for now and follow orders. I kept reminding myself to take it one day at a time, one step at a time.

four

Zoey

RACE KEPT HIS ARM around me as we walked back through the corridors toward the library. I almost relaxed into him as we walked because my thoughts were wandering, but then I realized where that would lead. I felt my muscles tense at that realization. I shrugged his arm off, continuing to explain about the book I found. He stopped me.

"I know you don't want to, but we really should talk about it, Zoey. You know how I feel and what I want. I'm just asking you to share your thoughts and feelings with me." Wow, was he persistent. It was the same conversation we'd started a million times since I broke things off with him earlier in the year after giving him a second chance for the third time. He just wouldn't let it go. His reaction was exactly why I almost didn't go to him about the book in the first place.

"Race, I can't talk about that now. It's gonna have to wait. It's been four months; we shouldn't need to talk about it anymore. Besides, how many times have we broken up now? It's not going to work. You know it; I know it. Hell, Jack knows it. So just drop it. OK? This book is more important than us. I'm not sure how to explain it, or even how I know; I just do. Please trust me. If you help me figure this out, I promise I'll have this discussion with you. Fair enough?" I was talking faster than usual, trying to cover up my discomfort at the sudden topic change. I just wanted to get back to the library and figure out the deal with that book.

I could tell by his face that he wasn't convinced I was honest. "Fair enough. So we'll have dinner and talk as soon as this business with the book is sorted out." It wasn't a question. And he managed to slip his arm around my shoulder again and give me a bit of a hug. I can't say I didn't enjoy it—he was very charming; I'm just not ready to lose myself again. I shrugged him off again as we walked through the door to my office.

The book was just where I had left it, sitting there on my desk. I guess I had half expected it to get up and walk off since it was able to talk to me. The book was still open, and the pages emanated a slight glow that was brighter than before. When I looked at the page, I was in shock—it was blank again! Race seemed to be interested in the pages' glow but not so impressed that the pages were blank. He picked up the book and flipped through it skeptically.

"OK, Zoey, what's the deal? Were you just trying to get me alone? Because I'm fine with that." He placed the book back on my desk and moved closer, attempting to wrap his arms around me again.

I shook my head, put my hands up, and backed away from him quickly. "Come on, Race, I'm serious. Somehow this book changes, and it knows my name! How is that possible? It's 2000 years old. I'm not joking." The only thing that seemed to have stopped him from pursuing me was the fact that I was almost in tears. He never did handle me crying very well.

"Woah, slow down. We'll figure it out. I promise. Calm down. Take a breath. I didn't mean to upset you." Race seemed to be the only person who ever really considered my feelings, which was only sometimes. I took a deep breath, picked up the book, and looked at him.

"OK, sorry. This whole situation is just so weird." I held the book in my hand, opening it as I spoke. "I opened it, asked Calliope to let me read it, and..." The pages started to glow again. Words appeared as though someone was writing them at that moment. "This! This is what happened!"

"Wow, you weren't kidding! How did you do that?" Race grabbed the book and flipped it over, inspecting the front and back covers. "It has to be electronic, right? But how did you make it look so old, Zoey? And where is the circuit board? I can't find a panel to open it."

Well, at least now he believes me. Maybe we can figure this out after all. Once he was satisfied with his inspection of the book and was convinced there was no electronic component, we decided to sit down on the small couch in my office and read it. Of course, he used this as an excuse to put his arm around me again. It wasn't worth fighting about, especially when we needed to be close to both read the pages. I focused on the book in my lap and ignored Race.

FIVE

Ian

I'M GENUINELY SORRY I frightened you, Zenovia; that wasn't my intent. I've just been trying for months to convince you to open this book, and I got a little excited when you finally obliged.

We have much to do, and I fear not much time to accomplish everything. I'll need you to prepare. Gather what you need, and I will tell you about the mission.

But wait, I'm getting ahead of myself. Let me start at the beginning. My name is Ian, I am a wizard, and I need your help. But we'll get to exactly what that means soon enough. Allow me to explain what happened. When I was a teenager, my friends (Mike, Ed, Trent, Franklin) and I were obsessed with Dungeons and Dragons. Do you know what that is? I wonder if it still exists in your time. Anyway, it's a role-playing game, and we loved it. We had a running game and played every other weekend at one house or another.

Our last game was pretty intense, and well, it's the reason that I have sought you out. It was Halloween. The year was 1985. My friends and I had decided to camp out in a deserted mansion that Mike's dad owned. The place was creepy but in good repair. Mike's dad owned a construction company and often bought, remodeled, and sold houses and storefronts. But that isn't the point of the story.

We had a battle during our game—I'm not sure if you are familiar with the game or not, but you'll catch on—and I cast a spell to capture a demon. I spoke my casting words and rolled a natural twenty. It was exhilarating! We saw a burst of blue energy appear and dissipate, encompassing the room. We all thought Mike's dad was playing a joke on us. It had to be a trick. Magic wasn't real. Or so we thought. Naturally, we were terrified and ran to our homes, not wanting to be in that place any longer. It felt as though the house was possessed, though I'm not sure any of us would have said that at the time.

We found out later that my spell had opened a doorway to another dimension. Ultimately, I had set magic free on Earth. I am singularly responsible for all the misery and destruction that has happened. It was unintentional, but I have to find a way to fix it.

Of course, we didn't realize right away what had happened. A few days later, I had a vision of Mike with his hands up, looking confused while everyone around him seemed to be frozen. I thought it was a weird dream until it happened. I must have been just out of range of the freeze spell because it did not affect me. Seeing the future was fun for a while until my visions began to show me what our innocent game had done to the world as we know it. I later learned that I could have images of the future, past, or things occurring in the present time. It took a while to figure out what period the visions were from when they happened. I have to admit, I was terrified at first. Some days I still am.

Over the next few weeks, we found out that each of us in that room was touched by magic. I started looking for answers wherever I could. I read books about magic—history books that mentioned it; I talked to anyone and everyone who may have had a thought about it. I became more than a little obsessed with learning everything I could. I found a group of magicians or witches, depending on what term you prefer—they called themselves the Coven—who tried to help me by teaching me some spells to help with learning and control. It just wasn't enough. I needed to find a way to fix what I had done.

I found this book at a pawn shop; its hand-bound leather called to me and pulled me to take it home. Over the years, after the Change—as it came to be called—we tried, though unsuccessfully, to fix what we had done. I found a spell that would allow me to use the book to communicate with myself in the past. Unfortunately, it didn't work. I couldn't reach my past self, most likely because I could only go back to when I first acquired the book.

One night, I had a vision that showed me how to call out to the chosen one. In this vision, I saw you and knew you would be the one to set the world right again. You will be our savior. I know it's a lot to take in at once, but I need you to agree to this quest. Then I can give you the details in private. Yes, I know your friend has been reading this the whole time. However, I'm not sure why you felt you couldn't trust me. I guess you can never be too careful.

Anyway, I can't force you to help me. It's your decision. Please just let me know when you've made the decision, and we can discuss the plan. Or I can move forward with my backup plans.

SIX

Zoey

I COULDN'T BELIEVE WHAT we had just read. I could tell Race was having a hard time with it as well. "What kind of crazy trick is this?" he asked, standing up and pacing the small floor of my office. It was clear that he was upset. He tried to grab the book from me, but I pulled it to my chest and held it protectively.

"Let me at least scan it for magic to see what we are dealing with," Race insisted. I reluctantly handed the book over as he pulled out his scanner. I hung over his shoulder as he sat the text on the desk and began the scan. "This will only take a minute, and then we'll know what type of magic we're dealing with, or if I somehow missed the electronic element."

"I don't know, Race, but I don't think it's a trick. I think it's magic. I feel like Ian is telling the truth, and it seems he needs our help." The look on his face said he disagreed. I wasn't sure what I could do to convince him that I was right.

As soon as the scan was complete, the device let out a series of high-pitched beeps. My hypothesis was confirmed, and Race became livid. I snatched up the book, once again clutching it to my chest protectively. The device was not able to identify the exact type of magic that had been used in the book. I wasn't concerned about that. I had a magic book. And that magic book connected me to a wizard who wanted me to go on a quest to save the Earth. The excitement must have been written all over my face. With the way Race was looking at me, I'd be lucky not to get locked up.

"No way am I going to let you do anything that some crazy, possessed book says. I'll get rid of it." He reached over and tried again to take the book from me, but I moved it just out of his reach. I wasn't about to just hand it over. Finding this was the single most exciting thing that had ever happened to me in my whole life. I wasn't giving this book up that easily.

"Wait, just hear me out—" I pleaded. "Let me do some research and see if any of what Ian told us so far is in the history of Earth. If it is, we'll know it's not a game. Fair enough?" If he decided to take the book from me by force, it would be a good fight, but I was sure he would win. I don't even think I could beat him by fighting dirty. My only option was to keep dodging and try to convince him to see it my way. I was ready to bolt and hide if I had to. I just hoped it didn't come to that. The Head of Tech was kind of hard to hide from. He programmed all the locks on Calliope and knew how to override them. But I might be able to beat him to a shuttle. After all, I was faster.

"Zoey, I don't like you risking yourself like this. But I trust you, so I'll do what you want. For now. If I find out this is a trick someone is playing on you, though, I'm going to take care of it." Race didn't stick around to see if I agreed. He stormed out and slammed the door behind him. His response was what I expected, knowing how he felt about me. I knew he was angry, but I couldn't go after him to calm him down for once. If I did, I would give in, and the book would be gone, along with my chance for adventure.

As soon as the door closed behind him, I knew Race wasn't going to let me take this quest. "Ugh, I'm gonna have to talk to him. I just don't know how to explain that my feelings don't align with his plans for us."

The open book began to glow slightly. I looked at it and received an unsolicited opinion from Ian on my relationship with Race.

You really should handle it now rather than letting him think you will decide to obey. We both know you don't love him. It will be harder to leave if you don't tell him the truth. And I'm going to need you to go to Earth to seek the magical item that can end all of this. You see, my dear, you need to address this to complete your mission to save the world. I know your friend thinks it sounds crazy, but you know I'm telling the truth. Yes, I already know you've made your decision, just as I knew you didn't want him to know.

"Wait, did you just answer me? I'm truly losing my mind right now and talking to a book. Crazy. They're going to lock me up for sure." I closed the book, tucked it in my backpack, and proceeded to investigate the events Ian had just told us about. Just because Race wanted me to leave it alone didn't mean I was going to listen. I was beginning to realize that defying Race may have been more of a contributing factor in my decision to take Ian's mission than I initially thought.

I was practically flying from the adrenaline rush of fighting with Race. I couldn't sit still when he left, so after pacing my office for a few minutes while I tried to wrap my head around everything Ian had told us, I headed to my room to start gathering what I would need for my trip. I told myself I hadn't decided yet if I was going, but even I didn't believe me. Even Ian knew I was going. For that matter, Race probably knew I was going. It didn't matter, as long as I planned it out carefully. I would have to come back to the library to gather what books I thought would be helpful, but I wanted to deal with my personal belongings first. And I might even try to talk myself out of doing this because Race could be right. It probably was crazy to run off on a quest just because an enchanted book told me to. But maybe, just maybe, crazy was what I needed right now.

seven

Race

AFTER STORMING OUT OF the museum, I returned to my office, where I paced back and forth, staring at the communicator in my hand. I knew what I had to do—I just hoped the consequences would be what I expected. I couldn't believe what Zoey had found. He had warned me that this could happen, which was why I had been assigned to Calliope after my studies were complete. I was waiting for just this moment. I hoped that she would listen to me and leave it be. Of course, I knew her too well for that. If I hadn't fallen for her, I would have just taken the book by force. But as much as I suspected that she didn't return my feelings, I knew I could never harm her. I loved her and wanted us to be together. If she took the time to consider my offer, she would understand.

He would make her marry me, just to keep her safe and out of the way. I was sure I could talk him into that. But for now, I knew I had to make a call. As much as I didn't want to, I knew I had to report what had just happened. I rushed back to my quarters and then checked video surveillance on Zoey to make sure she was still in the library. I couldn't have her barging in on this conversation. I knew the chances of that were slim, but I had to be careful. I dialed the number I knew by heart on the disposable communicator I had hidden in my desk.

As it rang, I watched her pacing as though trying to talk herself into or out of a decision. I walked along with her. I wasn't sure if I wanted her to change her mind or not. Maybe I should agree to go with her on this mission and not return to Calliope. At this point, I didn't think I could talk her into taking me with her if she did leave. My reaction to the book and its request may have been a little over the top. If I went with her, I could win her over and protect her from the Chairman. She'd be safe. Or maybe I should just disconnect the call and let her go on her own. She might be safe if he didn't know she had left. Even as I had the thought, I knew it was ridiculous. No one was safe as long as the Chairman was free. I was proof of that. The war inside my head continued until I made my decision. Now I have to stick with it.

I heard the receptionist pick up the phone and started talking before she could say a word. "This is Race. I need to speak with the Chairman. It's urgent." Without a comment in response, I was placed on a brief hold, and just when I thought the line had gone dead, I was met with a curt reply.

"This had better be good news. I do not take kindly to interruptions. You know this. Tell me." His voice was harsher than it had been the last time we spoke. I had to keep my cool, or I knew I'd never get what I wanted.

I paused for a second to keep my voice from cracking. "Yes, sir. It is important. It's about Zoey. She found it, the book you've been searching for. She has it, and it's just as you suspected—the wizard uses it to communicate with her. I tried to talk her out of helping the wizard, and when that failed, I tried to take the book from her, but she wouldn't let me. I didn't want to hurt her physically, so I gave in. What should I do?"

"Do nothing. I will arrive in the morning and handle this myself. Do not make anyone aware of my arrival. Watch the girl closely, boy."

"Yes, sir. Of course. Will you need anything for your stay? I will make sure your rooms are ready, and I will not alert anyone. I look forward to seeing you, sir."

He cut the call off without responding to my question or saying "goodbye." I had a lot to do and not much time to get it done. I turned off the monitor I had been watching Zoey on and walked out of my room to get started.

I had to use a back entrance to the Chairman's rooms so no one would know he was coming. I usually would have delegated the cleaning and preparation of rooms to someone else, but this was too important. I was planning to defy my boss and felt like this was the least I could do. I stripped and remade the bed, made sure the bathroom was clean and stocked, and then headed to the kitchen. I checked the food synthesizer to ensure it was working correctly and then left the same way I had entered. Not one single person on Calliope would even know I had been there.

I was too distracted to watch Zoey on the monitor when I returned to my room. I needed something to take my mind off the situation. I pulled out my comm device and shot off a text to one of the women who liked to keep me company in Zoey's absence. She was good at keeping secrets, as well as entertaining me. I decided to shower and get comfortable while I waited for her. By the time I finished, she had let herself in and was waiting for me in my bed. I was hoping to be distracted, and it appeared she might be able to do just that.

EIGHT

Jack

AFTER CLEANING UP THE Holo and finishing my daily responsibilities, I went up to the gym and ran for a few miles to clear my head. I was used to being alone, but there were moments where I felt lonely lately. I pulled the band from my hair and let it cascade down my back in a dark curtain as I walked away from the track. I figured a shower and dinner might ease my mind. I wanted nothing more than to stop hiding from those closest to me, but I knew it was for the best. I had to maintain appearances to stay in a position to protect my family, even if they weren't blood.

I ran into Race on my way back to my room from the gym. "Hey, man, what's up? You wanna get something to eat?" He was rushing around like he had something going on. "Nah, I don't have time right now. Some stuff came up, and I have to take care of it. You go without me." It wasn't like him to turn down food. "Are you OK? What happened with Zoey's problem earlier?" The look he gave me said it all.

He was upset with her and didn't want to talk about it. It seemed like there was something else going on with him as well. "It's fine. I took care of her problem. She'll be fine. We're working things out. I'll always take care of her." And with that, he walked away. It wasn't unusual for him to act this way when they were fighting. You'd think they had just broken up again the way he was acting. I'm sure he would have told me about that, especially since he had just told me earlier today that they were getting back together and then insisted as much just now. I figured if I were going to figure out what his problem was, I'd have to go straight to his usual source of upset, Zoey.

I found her in the library, acting strangely as well. "Hey, Zo, do you know what's up with Race? He's acting weird." She was digging through stacks of books, making different stacks and mumbling to herself. She barely looked up when I came in and spoke to her. I walked across the room and touched her arm. She jumped as though I had hit her.

"Oh! Jack, you scared me. What are you doing here? You don't usually come to the library. Is something wrong?" She tried to hide the guilt, but it was painted all over her face. As a master of hiding the truth, I was usually pretty good at picking up lies and shame.

"Do you want to talk about it?" I figured I'd give her a chance to tell me what was bothering her.

One look at my face and she broke. "I can't stay here. Race doesn't want me to leave. It's a long story. Please don't say anything to him."

I pulled her into a hug, wiping the tears from her cheeks. "It's OK. Just take a breath, and talk to me. What do you mean you have to leave? Where will you go?" I couldn't stand the thought of losing her any more than I wanted to deal with Race if she left. She hugged me back, composed herself, and then pulled away. It felt like she was saying "goodbye."

"I'm sorry, Jack. Of course, I'm not leaving. I just meant that I couldn't be with Race, and he doesn't understand. I need him to move on. But he keeps pushing for us to be together, and I just can't." I knew she was only telling me half the truth, but I didn't push. If it were something major, she'd tell me. She always did. Except for this time—I already knew what was wrong; I just couldn't tell her.

After striking out with Race and Zoey, I headed to dinner alone and then back to my room. After making sure no one was in the hall, flipping on the video jammer, and disabling the override to the door lock so I couldn't be disturbed no matter what, I dug the secure comm device out of the bottom of my closet. I knew the living quarters weren't supposed to have cameras, but I also knew Race and was convinced he'd had my room bugged. I wasn't sure what he suspected, but I couldn't take any chances. Once I was confident I couldn't be overheard, I flipped open the comm and called the only number programmed into it. Two rings later, and my call was answered.

"What's wrong? You know you can only use this number for emergencies. Is she hurt? What is it, Jack? Do I need to come back?" The familiar voice made me smile, even with its impatient tone. "Calm down, Mama Bear. You don't need to come back yet unless you just want to. She's OK. It's not that kind of emergency. Though I'm sure they've been fighting again. If he weren't my best friend, I would have already taken care of that part. But I think something is going on, and I need to know what you want me to do about it." I could feel the tension on the other end of the line dissolve, and the response was more relaxed.

"OK, I'm better now. Please fill me in. What has that boy done now?" Since I wasn't sure what Race and Zoey had been fighting about, I couldn't explain that part.

"Well, she finally opened the book. It was tough to feign indifference after your stories about that thing. There were so many questions I wanted to ask her. How did you know about the book, anyway? I think that's what they're fighting about, at least in part. I couldn't get a straight answer out of either of them, though. He said they're getting back together, and she said she couldn't stay here. She tried to cover with an explanation that she can't be with him, but I think Zoey meant that she's leaving. I'm fairly certain it has something to do with that book. Is that something you can explain?"

There was a slight hesitation before I got a response. "You know I've already told you too much. I can't give you any more info on the book. Did Zoey accept the quest? What else could they be fighting about if not that? I know it's difficult, but I need you to keep your cover. She can't know that you are working for me. This is all going to be impossible to explain as it is without adding that to it. Please. You promised." The voice was authoritative until the end. There was a hint of desperation along with the reminder that I had given my word. It was well-known that I did not break my word. I never gave it freely, so I meant it when I did. And keeping Zoey safe was the only reason I was still on Calliope. I'd been given several opportunities to leave for better jobs and better locations. I stayed because I gave my word.

"I'm not going back on my word. You know me better than that, or at least you should by now. I can't say for sure that Zoey accepted the quest, but it did appear that way. As for what else they could be fighting about, well, several things come to mind. For example, Race is constantly insisting they are getting back together when it's obvious to anyone and everyone that she doesn't feel the same about him. I'm not even sure he feels that way about her. I think he just wants a trophy, honestly. And she would give him a status boost. It's probably good that she doesn't know that."

There was a chuckle from the other end of the line. "True. If Zoey knew, we'd all be in danger. There's so much I should have told her. All I wanted was to keep her safe. Thank you for letting me know there may be an issue. Please continue to watch and report what you think I need to know. You will be richly rewarded." And just like that, the line went dead. I hid the secure comm back in the bottom of my closet, where it wouldn't be discovered.

Even though it was late, I knew sleep wouldn't come. I headed back to the gym and opted for a swim to relax. After an hour, I was still on edge. I changed into my shorts and shoes and headed for the track. If I couldn't swim my nerves away, I'd run it out. I sprinted around the track until my legs felt like jelly, and I couldn't take any more. My mind wasn't at ease, but my body was exhausted. I went back to my room and collapsed on the bed, falling asleep as soon as my head hit the pillow.

Nine

Zoey

I wasn't sure why I had decided to believe Ian and disregard Race's concerns over the quest laid before me. It was not the most reasonable decision. And if anything, I have always been good. Perhaps that's why I decided to chase down a mysterious magical item on a planet that was half dead. It was as if it wasn't a decision at all, but an unseen force was pulling me to follow Ian's words and ignore Race. Was it my feelings for him, or lack thereof, causing me to make rash decisions? I didn't think so. I felt like I had to do this, just as I had to breathe to stay alive. It didn't matter anyway because my mind was made up. I was going, and nothing could stop me. And I would be going alone.

I had wanted to talk the whole thing over with Jack when I ran into him, but I couldn't bring myself to say the words. I was scared he'd try to talk me out of it, or worse, that he'd try to go with me. Would that have been such a bad thing? Maybe I should go back and ask him about going. I couldn't, though. I couldn't ask one of my best friends to give everything he's worked for up just to go with me on a crazy quest that may be for nothing. Only then did the realization hit me.

Something inside warned me that if I left the space station, I would be giving up everything I've ever known. I realized I'd never be allowed to return to Calliope 127 if I left this way. But I also knew I'd never be granted permission for this trip. The council would never allow a sabbatical to search for some item a book told me to seek out—even if they believed me when I said that it was the only way to save the planet below us. I took one last look around my room, as I had just done not fifteen minutes earlier in the library.

I knew if I took my ID card, I could be tracked instantly. The ID was multi-functional, serving as an identification card, a key card for work, and living quarters access. It also carried credits earned and a tracking chip to prevent people from skipping job assignments. I knew that this one card took the place of many on Earth in the past from my research. We used them every day and had to make sure we were never without them. It was one of the space stations' requirements and part of the reason I knew I'd never be allowed to come back. I would have no way to prove who I was and no money. People on the space station got locked up for tampering with or destroying cards. This thought terrified me, and I hesitated as I carefully removed my lanyard and tucked it under some clothes in the bottom of a drawer.

I needed to pack quickly and figure out how I would get on the shuttle without my ID card. Luckily, my bag was enchant-ed and would hold everything without making it evident that I wasn't coming back. I double-checked my bag to make sure I didn't forget anything important. I could get by with a day trip to the surface, but I wasn't authorized for an overnight. I scheduled the journey from my room, hoping they didn't require my ID when I boarded the shuttle. Plus, I had to be extra careful since today wasn't my leisure day, and I knew if I were caught, I would probably be locked in my room for a while. I had never done anything remotely dishonest, so this felt like I was breaking all the space station laws. I knew the consequences of my actions, but was I brave enough to accept them? Would I falter when the time came to show strength? I had to be brave; I was the only chance Earth had for survival. Why did Ian's words ring so true for me? I had to find out.

So, under the guise of a simple day trip, I was going to leave everyone I knew. Was I going to do this? That thought crossed my mind as I grabbed my bag and paused at the door. Yes, I was. I was going to be the one who saved Earth.

And given that I had no idea who or what I was looking for or where to find it, I was confident it would take more than a day. I would call it a day trip if questioned about it but wasn't exactly sure what I would say about the fact that I was leaving in the middle of the night. I would try to explain that and how I lost my ID, though I was confident it wouldn't work. I double-checked my bag, again, to make sure I didn't forget anything important.

I had left the letters for Race and my parents in my room. I knew he'd go in there as soon as he realized I didn't intend to return. The letter to my parents explained why I left and requested that they forgive me for running off like this. I didn't give them many details but said that Race expected marriage, and I craved adventure. My soul wanted to travel to the places I'd read about.

On the other hand, my letter to Race was the most challenging thing I had ever been forced to write. I knew Ian was right, and if I didn't take care of it now, I would end up stuck in a marriage I didn't want. I would be expected to give up everything I'd worked so hard for just because Race preferred his women subservient. There was no way I could ever be happy in that life. I wanted freedom. I'd always done what was expected, right up to the day I broke things off with Race. Now I had to end it permanently.

Race

I WOKE EARLY THE following day. I knew the Chairman would alert me to his presence when he arrived, so I went about my day as usual. It was my job to make sure everything dealing with technology worked correctly, so needless to say, I stayed busy. I wanted to see Zoey, but with the way she had blown off any talk of our relationship last night, I knew that was a bad idea. When she got in these moods, she would avoid me for days. Even if I could corner her, she'd just make up some excuse about a book that was more important than our conversation and disappear again. I could try to wait her out, but I wasn't even sure that would work this time. I would just have to wait until the Chairman came. Once he had the book, maybe I would convince her that we were meant to be together. Or perhaps the Chairman would just make her marry me, even though she didn't think that's what she wanted.

I knew I could make her love me if she'd just give me a chance. She could be so stubborn. That's probably why I'd been in love with her since we were kids. I tried everything to get close to her and had even convinced her to date me for a bit. I wasn't sure what had gone wrong. It was like she woke up one morning and decided she didn't want to be with me. I think her feelings for me scared her, and she wasn't able to admit it. It's not like I was lonely; I had plenty of other girls on the side that I had managed to hide from her. But Zoey was my number one, and they all knew it. I mean, yeah, I mostly wanted her because of her connections, especially those she didn't even know about. But that shouldn't matter. At least I liked her. I wasn't used to not getting what I wanted, so this situation didn't sit well.

Just because I couldn't see Zoey didn't mean I couldn't check on her with the video surveillance. I pulled up the library on the monitor in front of me. "Oh, shit!" The second I saw it, I knew I was in trouble. The library was empty, the lights were off, and the door was locked. It appeared to be closed, which was odd, given that Zoey never got sick or took a day off. It was one of the great things about her family. Their planet had been harsh but beautiful and created healthy beings, a strength which somehow must have passed through the blood since Zoey didn't grow up there. Something was wrong.

I pulled up her room on the monitor—there weren't supposed to be cameras in the living quarters, but I was in charge of tech, so there wasn't anyone to stop me from installing a few in certain places. And I liked to keep an eye on what was mine. Just like the library, her room was empty. It was spotless, with the bed meticulously made and what looked like two envelopes sitting on her pillow. Zoey being gone was bad, so very bad for me. I had to investigate before the Chairman got here. I had a feeling he wasn't going to like this. "Oh, no, no, no. Please be there. Please be late. Please don't be gone." I knew my words were pointless, as I was sure she wouldn't be anywhere on Calliope.

I rushed to the library, and it was, as suspected, closed. I had wanted the cameras to be wrong, but they weren't. I went down the hall to Zoey's room and found it unlocked and empty. After a bit of searching, I realized she had taken all her belongings but had left everything I had given her behind. I slammed the boxes at the walls; everything was broken by the time I was finished. There were two letters on the bed, one addressed to me and one to her parents. I opened mine immediately and read it three times just to be sure of what it said.

Dear Race,

I know by now you've realized I'm not coming back. You probably figured it out the moment you walked out of the library. You told me that you didn't want me to go, and I'm genuinely sorry for doing this. It's my destiny to go on this quest. There was nothing you could have done to stop me. Try not to worry. I'll be fine. I promise. You really couldn't have stopped me, so don't beat yourself up about it.

And I know I owe you a conversation as well. I'm sorry doesn't begin to cover it, but there's nothing I can do at this point to make it better. This will have to do:

It's not easy to say this, but although I care deeply for you, it's not in the way you want it to be. I don't want to quit my job and be your mate, raising our offspring and tending to our living quarters. That has never been my desire. I know it's yours because you've told me several times. You deserve to find someone who wants those things too.

Until today, I wanted nothing more than to stay here at Calliope and run the museum. You know books have always been my passion. But if there's even a slight chance that I can fix this world, I have to try. And even if you had agreed to let me keep my job, I couldn't marry you. We are just too different. Your culture and mine just don't mesh well. I know I should have told you this years ago, but I had hoped you'd find someone else and move on.

And to be perfectly honest with you, I want to be free. I want to travel, to see all the worlds, to have my own life.

I hope someday you can forgive me. And I genuinely do hope you find the one to make you happy. Thank you for everything you've done for me. I trust you'll forward the other letter to my parents.

Thank you,

Zoey

I knew I was in trouble. I'd had one job to keep Zoey safe. OK, two jobs...to keep an eye on her and alert the Chairman if the book had been found. Where could Zoey have gone? I had to locate her, and fast...like before he arrived, fast. The Chairman was not a forgiving man, especially when you messed up a job. I might lose my head for this. Oh, man, this could get ugly, really fast. This situation was terrible, so awful. Could this day get any worse? How could she leave like that after I told her not to listen to the wizard? I didn't particularly appreciate being defied, but I was more worried about the Chairman's reaction.

I rushed to the library, hoping she had left the book behind. I knew there was no chance of her going on this mission without it. But that book was the only thing that could save my life at this point. It's not a good idea to disappoint the Chairman. When I had finished tearing the rooms apart, I called for a clean-up crew for the museum, library, and her room and then arranged for a temporary to cover the museum and library. I didn't find the book but was hopeful that it would turn up somewhere between the library and her quarters. I assigned crew members to search everywhere in hopes that she had just hidden it. They knew what they were looking for, but they had no idea why.

I went back to my office, where I pulled up travel logs for the shuttles that went to Earth daily. Sure enough, her name was on one of them. She didn't even try to hide it. Well, at least I would have a general location to give the Chairman.

The shuttle she had taken was going to Italy. With any luck, it was just a day trip, and she would be back tonight. But even I didn't believe that. As much as I hated to do it, I wiped the logs. I didn't want him to know the exact time she left. I would claim a tech glitch and buy her some time that way. Maybe I wouldn't tell him where she was headed either. There was still a chance I could find her before he did, explain that I had protected her, and convince her to marry me. Right? This wasn't the end, just because she left. I would come up with a plan. I still had time. I tried so hard to convince myself that my wild thoughts were true that I almost believed them. Almost.

All I could do was wait, push down my fears, and hope for forgiveness that I was sure would not be granted. I knew he would arrive soon. I briefly considered running. In the end, I decided against it. There was nowhere I could go to escape him. All I could do was try to give Zoey a head start with no safe place to hide. Maybe she really could fix what had happened to our planet. I had my doubts, but she seemed so convinced. For once in my life, I decided to put someone else first. Unfortunately for me, I knew it would cost me my life. I told myself that I was making the ultimate sacrifice for love and that I wouldn't give him the satisfaction of fighting back when the time came.

Chairman

As I ARRIVED AT the space station, I felt something amiss before the doors closed behind me. It was a disturbance in the energy, and I had a feeling I knew what I would find. But I would give the boy a chance to explain before I doled out his punishment.

I headed straight to Race's office, bypassing my quarters, the library, and Zoey's quarters. I busted through the locked office door without pausing. He looked as though he was trying to hide his fear, but he wasn't doing it very well. I stopped just inside the door and waited for him to speak first.

"Sir, I didn't know you had arrived." My presence caught him off guard; his face told me as much. I relished the feeling of respect and fear from those who served me. I chose a mask of indifference rather than the smirk I wanted at that moment.

"Explain." I truly hoped he had a good excuse for whatever had him so spooked about my visit. I knew better because there were no good excuses. Failure would not be tolerated. This boy's fate had already been decided, probably when he accepted the mission to watch Zoey and report back when she found the book. Besides, I would leave no one to challenge me. And none would know the lengths I went to for the power I was seeking.

He stammered a little before spitting out words. "I, sir, I'm sorry. She left either late last night or early this morning. She took a shuttle down to Earth; the records are unclear about whether it left last night or this morning. The logs glitched, the locations and the timestamps were erased. I checked her room and found this. I didn't open it." I was impressed that his thoughts were as coherent as they were, given the intimidation that was radiating off him. I knew he was lying to me about the glitch, but he was shielding his thoughts pretty well. I couldn't determine if he had deleted them or if it had been someone else. He then handed me a handwritten note. I cocked an eyebrow at him, then I read it.

Dear Mama and Daddy,

I'm sorry for just running off like this. I know you wanted me to stay here where it's safe. I hope you can forgive me. It's been so long since I've seen you. I've grown and changed so much in the past few years. I know it will be hard for you to accept, but I'm an adult now and can make my own decisions. All I ever wanted was to make you proud of me. I hoped to do that by running the museum and library, but I must go. Please hear me out--

I've been chosen for a quest. I found a magical book. I know how that sounds, but it's true. Ask Race—he will tell you. A wizard owns the book, and he needs my help. I don't know if it's safe to give you too many details, but I will tell you that I have to go to Earth for a while. I'm not sure exactly where this quest will take me, but please know that everything you taught me has prepared me to do this. I will be successful. I will save the Earth. I will make you proud.

I chose to take this quest on my own. I can't just stay on Calliope for the rest of my life. I need adventure. I need freedom. And no matter how much he wants it, I just can't marry Race. I don't love him, and I can't pretend. Please understand. This was a difficult decision to make. I hope that someday you can forgive me for running off.

I know you are very busy, so please forgive Race for being the bearer of bad news. He didn't have a choice. I would have told you myself, but I haven't heard from you in so long, and I have no idea how to find you. It's the one thing Race wouldn't do for me. I know your work is critical, so I never pushed for it. Please don't worry; I'll be safe. I promise. I love you both very much, and I hope to see you soon.

Love you lots and lots,
Your Little Schmoopsie

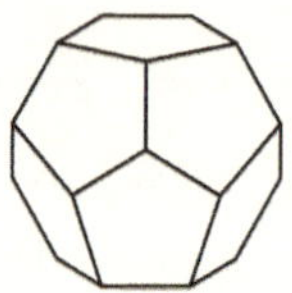

After reading the note, I knew that she had taken the book with her. But I wasn't sure if Race knew. I felt he needed to be tested. I didn't look up from the paper as I spoke.

"And where is the book?" I asked him, already knowing what his response would be.

"I, uh, I searched the library, sir, and couldn't find it. I, uh, I guess she must have taken it with her. But I have crews searching just in case it's hidden. Is it a big deal?" He seemed scared of how I would react, but not enough so to cower. It was impressive.

I should have known that he wouldn't understand the gravity of the situation. "Insolent boy. How could you let her go? Why did you not make sure she couldn't leave?" I made sure not to raise my voice. I had learned that speaking softly was much more intimidating.

"I had no idea she would leave, sir. She's never been anywhere but here. She's never even mentioned Earth before. I didn't expect her to go. I thought she would stay here because I asked her to. I told her not to listen to the book."

"I see. And what do you think I should do about this?" I wondered if he would know how he would be punished. Would he expect my reaction?

He hung his head in shame. "You must do what you see fit, sir. A mistake this large must be addressed." At that moment, I knew he had accepted his fate. He knew what was about to happen and would not do anything to stop it.

At least he knew he deserved what was to come next. I used my magic to grab him by the throat, slowly cutting off his airway. I was somewhat impressed with the amount of control he had over himself in this situation. He instinctively started to fight against the pressure on his throat. His eyes were wild with fear. He looked at me, then he stopped himself from fighting, allowing me to choke the life out of him slowly.

I almost felt bad about what I was doing, but then I remembered that it would be repeated if failure was not addressed immediately. I decided to let Race's death be a lesson to others who would not take me seriously. Watching him die was satisfying but would have been more so had he tried to fight for his life. I left his limp, lifeless body lying on the floor and departed the space station. No one else had even known I was there. I made sure they never would.

TWELVE

Jack

I sensed the power surge coming from Race's office and instantly knew what had happened. The pain of it stopped me in my tracks. I knew I would get there too late to stop it. I ran anyway, from my office two floors up, down the stairs, to his office door. What I saw from the partially opened door was paralyzing. I blinked back the tears as I punched the buttons on the door panel that would call security. I knew better than to touch anything, though I knew there would be no evidence of what happened. I sat outside the door staring at his lifeless eyes until the guards came.

There were five security personnel. One of them, whose name tag said Stephen, checked the cameras to prove I hadn't been the one to kill him and then let me say goodbye to my best friend. I hugged his limp body to my chest and promised him I would avenge his death. Then I watched as two of the guards loaded him onto a stretcher and wheeled him away while Stephen and two others began searching for clues as to who could have done this.

I stopped them for a moment to make sure they had contact information for Race's parents. I knew there was no way I could make that call myself. We hadn't spoken since they retired to the Gamma Quadrant. The news would be better coming from someone they didn't know.

I walked back to my room in a daze. I couldn't believe Race was gone. It wasn't until I put my hand on the door panel to unlock it that I realized I had to be the one to tell Zoey. I knew she wasn't in love with him, but as close as the three of us were, I knew she'd be devastated. I turned my back on the open door and headed to the museum.

The doors were open when I got there, and it looked as though a tornado had ripped through every book in the place. The second I saw it, I knew Zoey wasn't there. I had tampered with the shuttle logs and systems so identification cards wouldn't be requested if she decided to leave in the middle of the night. It appeared as though she had accepted the mission and had left. At that moment, I knew that her decision had been what cost my best friend his life. She wasn't responsible for his death, but she was the indirect cause. I stood in the doorway and let the tears fall. After a few minutes of allowing myself to grieve, I knew I had to get back to work. The mission didn't end just because someone died and someone else took off.

I made my way back to my room once more. After going inside, I took the usual precautions for a private conversation, even though the person I'd always thought I was hiding from was no longer an issue. I disabled the door lock to avoid potential overrides from unwanted company, jammed the cameras, and then pulled out the comm device and made a call. Once again, it was answered after two rings.

"Two calls in one week—now I know something is wrong. What happened?" The voice held concern this time.

I did my best to keep the emotion out of my voice as I answered. "She took the mission. She's gone. And he's dead—strangled, no evidence at the scene. At least now we know whom he was working for. No one else had a reason to kill him. It had to be the Order."

There was a solemn pause before the response came. I could have sworn I heard a sniffle as well. "Well. It's good she took the mission. I am sorry about your friend. I wish he had been on the right end of all this. Thank you for the notification. I'll be in touch for your next steps." I heard the faint click as the call was disconnected.

I finally allowed myself to collapse into my grief on the floor. It was like losing my parents all over again. The realization hit me that I was alone again. With Race dead and Zoey gone, I had no one left. Since it was just me now, I decided I would worry about the mission tomorrow. Tonight was for memories. I pulled out a bottle of whiskey and downed half of it. I'd be strong tomorrow. Tonight I'd be drunk and alone. So very alone.

I woke in the morning, still on the floor with the empty whiskey bottle on the floor next to me. My head throbbed, and I felt sick, but I knew it would pass quickly. Garlax had pretty strong constitutions so that a hangover wouldn't slow me down for long. I showered, then went down three floors to security to see if they had found anything in the investigation.

Stephen was on duty again, at his desk this time. I walked straight over to his desk, pulled up a chair, and sat silently. He looked up from his paperwork, nodded, and then went back to it. Once he was finished with his notes, he stacked the papers neatly and placed them in a folder.

"I wondered how long it would be until you showed up." Stephen's eyes held compassion and maybe a bit of pity. I didn't let it phase me.

"Then you know what I want," I replied.

He nodded. "We don't have anything. No evidence, no witnesses, no prints. Nothing." His face told me that he'd expected me to be surprised.

"I know." I did my best to keep my expression neutral.

Stephen's jaw dropped at my response. "What do you know? Do you know who did this? What evidence do you have?"

I couldn't tell him without putting him in danger. "I don't have any evidence, but I'm sure I know who did it. I won't accuse anyone without proof. But I'm working on that."

He smiled knowingly at me, then reached in his desk drawer. He pulled out a thick envelope with my name on it, written in Race's quick scrawl. I had no idea what might be inside but imagined I'd be finding out. He handed the envelope over to me, and I looked it over before opening it. There were no other marks on it except for my name.

"It was hidden in his room with a disposable comm and some blank logs. It didn't feel right to open it without you." He responded.

"Thank you. I appreciate that. Let's find out what this is, shall we?" I slid my finger under the lip of the envelope, pulled it open, and put my hand inside. I pulled out a stack of bills and a handwritten letter. I hadn't seen paper money in person before; the space station worked on a credit system tied to our identification cards. Stephen's eyes got big when he saw the cash. I guessed he knew what it was. I handed it over for him to count and turned my attention to the letter.

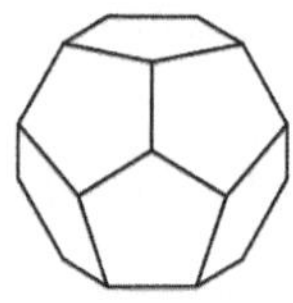

Jack,

You're the best friend I've ever had. If you're reading this, they've killed me. And I probably deserved it for what I've done. As many times as I wanted to take it back, I couldn't. I want you to know everything I did was because I thought it was in Zoey's best interest at first. By the time I realized I was wrong, it was too late. I got in too deep. There was no way out. I can't begin to apologize for lying to both of you or for the awful things I've done.

Promise me you'll keep her safe no matter what. Take this cash and get away from Calliope; go somewhere else and start over. It's better this way. I couldn't keep her safe here. I just didn't realize it in time.

Please find her. I know she'll go off after some magical quest item for that wizard, but if you don't locate her, she'll get herself killed. She deserves better than that. I knew she was going to go the minute I walked out of the library yesterday. I hope I'm wrong, but if she hasn't left yet, she will.

And I know you've been investigating me for a while. It's been hard to keep everything from you. Do you remember when we were kids in Miss Miller's class? It was so hard to keep that a secret too. But we found a way.

You'll find what you need if you look in the right place. Names, dates, missions, and details I could have been killed just for writing down. I guess it's too late for that, huh? Just promise you'll get justice for her sake, not mine. I got what I deserved. And in the end, I know I'm giving my life up for hers.

Thank you for always being the friend I needed. You were way better to me than you ever should have been.

I love you, man.

Race

Jack

I COULDN'T BELIEVE WHAT I had just read. Race confirmed everything and had the evidence I needed to help take the Chairman down. I just had to figure out where he had hidden it. "I'm guessing the location of the files has something to do with what he said about your class when you were kids?" I had almost forgotten Stephen was sitting there. His idea made sense.

"You're probably right. Now I just have to figure out what he's talking about." I took the letter with me, leaving the cash with Stephen, who put it back in the envelope and placed it back in his desk drawer. I had no use for it; I wasn't going anywhere except to catch a murderer.

I re-read the letter a few times, trying my best to remember when we were in Miss Miller's class. I didn't remember many details about our years in elementary school. I wasn't sure what secret we had back then. It had to be a clue. I just had to figure out what it meant. The only thing that stood out to me about our school time was when I got in trouble. We were seven, and I got in a fight with an older boy. I'm not even sure what the argument was about, though I could guess. I was still pretty tender back then about losing my parents. I didn't have much control over my temper, and it didn't take much to set me off.

I ran away. Race had found me in the vent outside the cargo hold. That had to be where he had hidden the files. I tucked the letter in my pocket and sprinted to the cargo hold on the floor below security. I was out of breath when I got there. I doubled over with my hands on my knees, trying to catch my breath. I realized I probably should have brought my camera jammer with me so no one would know our hiding spot. Then I decided it didn't matter now that Race was gone. I wouldn't need it anymore.

I pulled the cover off the vent, much the same way as I had as a child. Back then, I had been angry and scared. I guess the past does repeat itself. I had to do this. I had to bring the Order to justice. For Race, for Zoey, for everyone. Once the cover was off, I stuck a hand inside and felt around. He did well to hide it there. I had to reach down to my shoulder to find it. I wrapped my fingers around it and pulled out a thumb drive. It had a fingerprint sensor on it, and I knew he would have set it so only I could access it. He was creative like that. I replaced the cover and headed back to my room more casually than I had arrived.

Once I was in my room, I pulled out my handheld computer with my usual precautions in place. The thumb drive plugged into it, and I unlocked it with my left middle finger. Race wasn't kidding when he said it had everything I would need. There were names, dates, mission details, the works. There were a few additional files that were coded, and he hadn't included a cipher. Those would take some time to figure out. I would have to search Race's room and see if I could find the key to his code. If I couldn't find it, I'd have to write a program to decode it.

After reviewing the other files, some of my suspicions were confirmed, and I learned some new things. I would have to be careful who I trusted. And I would have to warn Stephen to do the same. His knowledge of this information put him in as much danger as it did me. I made a backup copy of the files, hid it, and then headed out to discuss the whole mess with Stephen. I just hoped I wasn't too late.

I raced down the hall and practically jumped down the three flights of stairs to get to the security office. I paused at the door to compose myself and then walked in. Stephen wasn't at his desk. "Hey, where'd he go?" I gestured to the empty desk, and the guard just shrugged. I'm guessing he wasn't very good at his job. I walked back out and weighed my options. I could access personnel records and find out where Stephen's quarters were, or I could wait it out. Maybe his shift was over, and he went home. It would probably be a good idea to wait and see if he turned up, rather than dragging any more people into this mess. And I still had to check in with Mama Bear. She needed to know what she was up against. We needed to regroup and formulate a plan. I walked back into the security office, asked the guard on duty to have Stephen call me when he got back in, and then headed back to my room.

I took the usual precautions and then called in. Two rings, and then an answer, as usual. "You have something?" The voice was anxious and laced with a bit of sadness.

"Yeah, I have something." I took a minute in silence to work out exactly how to word what was coming next. "Race left me files with details of everything he was involved in. I have names, dates, mission details...the whole nine yards. It should be enough to put them all away."

"That's fantastic. Why do you not sound excited about it? What aren't you telling me?" The voice was getting a little paranoid now.

"I don't know how to tell you this, Mama Bear." I paused.

"Just tell me, Jack. It can't be that bad." Her response was impatient. I grunted a chuckle.

"They were the ones who took your husband. And they still have him. They were doing experiments, and it appeared that he might have been a subject, along with a couple of hundred other people."

She gasped in shock. "You mean Dmitri is alive? I thought he died in that explosion. How could Race have been involved? I don't understand how he could be a part of such a thing." I could hear the tears in her voice as she spoke. It was hard news to swallow. I knew her heart was as broken as mine had been when I read the documents.

"There's more, Mama Bear, but I think we should wait to discuss it. We need to formulate a plan to capture them and bring them all to justice. We still don't know who their leader is. Race wasn't high enough in rank to find out everything. I wish he had confided in me, so I could have helped him get out." My voice broke, and I knew the tears would come again.

"Jack, it's OK to hurt. It's OK to break down if you need to. Grieving doesn't happen instantly. I know that he was like a brother to you. We can discuss the rest later. Take some personal time, and then contact me again. I'll see what we can come up with on my end as far as a plan." With that, she disconnected the call. I couldn't help but wonder if it was because she was hurting as badly as I was right now. I was pretty sure I already knew that was it.

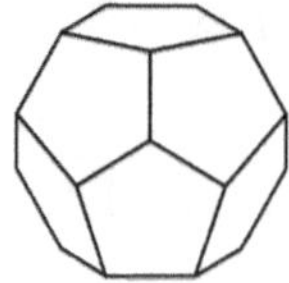

The following day, I went back down to security to check on Stephen. He seemed like a good kid...just in the wrong place at the wrong time. I needed to warn him to watch his back. When I got there, a different guard was at the desk. This one was a woman, and her name tag said Marlene. "Where's Stephen?"

Her face told me everything I needed to know. "Stephen's body was found this morning. It looked like he'd been tortured before whoever it was finished him off. I probably shouldn't have told you that, but I know you were asking about him yesterday, and you seem like a good guy." She didn't seem to think I could have done it, which was good for me. I wanted to see them find who did this. I had a list of suspects, but I'd be putting everyone in danger if I shared it. For now, I would have to handle this myself. I thanked her for the intel, then turned to walk away.

She stopped me. "Hey, Jack?" I turned around. "Yeah?" She stood up, walked over to me, handed me an envelope, and walked back to her desk. I raised an eyebrow, and she put a finger to her lips. She had an idea of what got Stephen killed. I'd have to make it a point to talk to her alone, very soon.

I headed back to my room, though I should have been reporting to work. I decided to send a message to my subordinate, Jeff, and let him know I'd be taking a personal day. Being the boss had some advantages. And Jeff was more than capable of handling things for one day. After sending my message, I secured myself in my room and laid out everything I had so far. Within half an hour, I had a paper trail spread across the floor and pages tacked to the wall.

Race's intel went more in-depth than I had thought initially, but I still wasn't any closer to figuring out who the big bad guy was. The identity of the Chairman was a mystery as well. I had the names of all the operatives working on Calliope and of the ones who just visited from time to time. It wasn't enough to figure out who had killed Stephen. I knew I could find out with some digging. I needed to have everything laid out before I stirred things up.

FOUrTeen

Zoey

IAN DESCRIBED THE ITEM he was convinced would be able to fix everything as a stellated dodecahedron. When I looked it up, I discovered the object looked like a star with points all over it. I had previously seen one in a book of drawings by Leonardo da Vinci. He said it would fit in the palm of my hand. I wasn't sure how this shape would help us, but Ian was convinced that this particular one was potent. He mentioned that his research indicated this was what the item looked like, but he also said he couldn't be sure. It could also look like a random twelve-sided die. There was only one way to be sure, and that was to find it. However, he hadn't been able to pinpoint the location of it yet. But I guess it wouldn't be a quest if it were easy.

Once I had everything ready to leave, I grabbed my bag and took one last look around the library. I would miss this place. It was the first place that felt like home since Zyterra was destroyed. But I knew if I could find the dodeca, and if it genuinely held the answer, I had a chance to find a place to call home again. Maybe I could even save my home planet from its fate. I know...that's a lot of ifs on which to base a significant life decision. I couldn't help myself; I felt so drawn to the book.

A single tear slipped down my cheek as I turned to go. I had to move quickly to catch the shuttle. I managed to board just as the doors were closing and the announcements began over the loudspeakers. I sat there, staring wistfully out the window, impatiently waiting to make it to Earth and find out my next step. I kept checking my bag to make sure the book was still there, along with the other books I had "borrowed" from the library. It was late, and the shuttle bay was not crowded at all.

"Ok, Ian, I got on the shuttle. I'm heading down to Earth. Then what?" I flipped through the book as the shuttle flew toward the over-industrialized planet below. I spoke softly, almost to myself, to avoid getting strange looks for talking to a book. I couldn't help second-guessing myself. I hadn't left the space station since my parents brought me there for refuge. I wasn't scared to be on my own; I was more concerned that I would disappoint my parents.

I wasn't even sure I could talk to Ian that way or if our connection had to be initiated by him. Then the page started to glow softly, and I received my answer.

Zenovia, don't be afraid; I am with you every step of the way. You can ask questions aloud if you wish or write in the book, and I will do my best to answer everything.

Well, at least now I knew how the book worked for communicating. "So where am I going once I get to Earth? And please stop calling me that."

I'm sorry, you don't wish to be addressed by your name? What shall I call you then?

"My friends call me Zoey. Come to think of it, everyone has always called me Zoey. No one ever even knew my name was Zenovia. It's a complicated story that you wouldn't understand. Now stop avoiding my question...where am I going when we get to Earth?"

OK, I'll try to remember that. Wait, what? Avoiding...oh, Earth. Yes, well, when you get there, you'll need to head toward Greece. No better place to find a Greek demigod. I suppose the exact directions will depend on where this—what did you call it?—lands. It could be a short trip, or it could take a while.

"It's called a shuttle. According to the histories I studied, the Earth had shuttles in your time. How do you not know this?"

Well, to be fair, the space program had shuttles. Regular people didn't. They weren't something that just anyone could board and take a trip on. We really are from two different worlds.

"Tell me about it." And I closed the book, choosing silence for the remainder of my trip.

The shuttle landed at the depot in Italy. I did a pretty good job choosing a destination with no information about where

I was going. At least my trip to Greece wouldn't be as bad as if I ended up halfway around the world. Now I just had to find a bus or a boat to get me the rest of the way.

Once I was settled into the ferry boat, I pulled out the book and began to talk to Ian again. "I'm sorry for being short with you before. Will you tell me more?"

FIFTEEN

Ian

I DIDN'T REALIZE UNTIL it was too late that I was binding my soul to it by using the book to call to the future. I had cursed myself

to being trapped inside the book for eternity unless I could find a way to reverse the change.

I think it may be helpful if you know what happened to my friends after the change. I'll tell you each of their stories. Hopefully, what we went through will help you find what we need to fix this situation.

Mike told me about the first time his new powers showed themselves. It was the day after our game went wrong, so it was November 1. We had all gone home late the night before. Mike said he slept until around ten and then took a shower, got dressed and headed over to Trent's house. They had planned to shoot hoops at the court. (Wait, did you understand any of that? I don't have the most exact picture of where you are and what you have exposure to, so if something is confusing, just let me know) OK, so Mike drove over and picked Trent up. They started playing basketball, and as Trent went for a layup, he froze in mid-air. Mike wasn't sure exactly what happened, and it only lasted for about thirty seconds. Then Trent unfroze and continued his shot. Of course, Mike was dumbfounded and just stood there with his mouth open. Trent stopped and asked if he was alright, and Mike explained what had just happened. Trent decided it was a good idea for Mike to see if he could recreate the phenomenon. So, they walked around the park...Trent throwing the ball and Mike attempting to freeze it. Having just received the power the night before and not knowing about it, naturally, he had no control. They gave up and headed home. A couple of days later, it seemed easier for Mike to call on his power and use it for his purposes. Other than Ed, Mike had the most control over his ability.

Trent ended up with the power to read thoughts. That sounds pretty cool, right? I thought so too. He thought it was cool to talk to a pretty girl and instantly know what she was thinking. He thought it would be a cool party trick—I bet I can guess what you're thinking—but when he couldn't make it work the way he wanted, he got frustrated and gave up. It was an extremely fickle power. It seemed like the more he tried to ignore it, the more erratic it got. Trent could receive parts of thoughts or complete ones, but he never knew which he was getting. Then once the power started to corrupt everyone, it wasn't so cool. He became paranoid and withdrawn. We tried to help him, but since he could only get snippets of our thoughts, he misinterpreted our concerns for intentions to get rid of him. I felt so badly for him, having locked himself away in his room and refusing to see or speak to anyone. It's hard to say what happened to him because he cut off contact when he locked himself away. None of us ever saw or heard from him again.

By far, Ed's gift was the best for parties. He could create and control fire with his bare hands. We tried to get him to show it off, but he didn't like the spotlight. Lucky for us, Ed was always the most level-headed and chose to keep his power a secret from everyone but us. He showed us what he could do one night when we were all hanging out in his basement. Ed simply opened his hands, and flames appeared. He made them dance, grow and recede according to his will. Then he extinguished them and went on as if it had never happened. Ed seemed to have a natural calm that helped him with his power. I think he practiced the most to control it, well besides Franklin, that is. Ed was the only one of us who didn't let the power corrupt him. He was the best of us. From what I know of his story, he led a pretty dull life, hiding his ability from those who would abuse it.

That brings us to Franklin. His power was the most erratic. He could teleport but had no control over it. Besides Trent, the rest of us practiced and found a way to at least somewhat control ours. Franklin never managed to master his gift. The poor guy *spent hours, days, weeks even, trying to master his power. He would be in the middle of a conversation, and *poof* he was gone. He'd turn up across town in a random yard or pool. No amount of meditation or spell work made it any better. He was miserable. With that lack of control came fear, and for a good reason too. Six weeks after the change, he teleported into the lake while sleeping, and he drowned. Sadly, I had a vision of this after it happened, and while I couldn't save him, at least we knew he didn't even wake up as it occurred.*

I've already told you about some of my powers. I can receive visions of the past, present, and future. It took a while to find a way to separate them from my thoughts. I've also learned to call visions, though I still have no control over what they show me. And I received the ability to astral project myself in my sleep and have worked to expand it to my waking hours. Astral projection allows me to send my consciousness—my soul if you prefer—to a location separate from my body. It comes in handy for research. I've managed to become a somewhat accomplished sorcerer in addition to these gifts, creating spells and potions.

At this point, I should probably tell you about The Order of Orpheus. Because if I don't, you'll just find out on your own. I don't think it will be an issue just yet, but better safe than sorry. It is typically referred to as The Order. It is a secret society working under the authority of the government of Earth. Their goal is to collect and secure the most powerful magic. The government wants to keep the most powerful items and people for itself. It has a secure location underground where it hides these things and people. Of course, the government denies the existence of The Order, but I've seen it, so I know it's there. The Order is made up of highly trained wizards, so be careful. They aren't afraid to kill to get what they want. I'm terrified they will decide to come after the book. If they confiscated the book, I would have no way to communicate with you, and you wouldn't have the information you need for the quest. Please keep the book safe and out of sight when you are traveling. I hope you will take all necessary precautions and keep yourself safe as well. I cannot do this without you. Get some rest, and we will discuss this more later. I want you to be aware of the risks and take the necessary precautions.

sixteen

Zoey

"Wow, I can't believe you all went through that! I'm so sorry about Franklin! If we can find a way to fix this, do you think he will come back? Do you think we can fix this with the dodecahedron?" I didn't have the heart to tell him that I only understood part of what he had said. Fortunately, I had done some reading on Earth's history, so it wasn't all confusing. I'm not sure we could have managed if I hadn't understood anything he had said.

Ian didn't respond. I guess it was his turn to be upset. I felt horrible because I hadn't intended to hurt him. I was sure everything he'd been through with his friends weighed heavily on him. We sat in silence until the boat reached a port in Greece. I asked Ian who or what I was looking for here. He had said something about a Greek demigod earlier, but I wasn't sure who that was or when that was supposed to happen. He didn't seem to want to tell me much. When you're interacting with a book, it's hard to convey tone. I wasn't sure if he was still upset or just didn't have anything to say since he responded with just a name...*Kyro*.

I picked up the book and my belongings and exited the boat. I wandered the dock for a while, figuring out if Kyro was a person or a location. I stopped to help an older man who was struggling to get a crate onto his boat. He was probably eighty or so years old, with tufts of gray hair showing under his hat and a long gray beard covering his wrinkled face. He was so adorable; I had to help him. There was no way he would be able to lift that crate onto his boat. It was heavy, close to sixty pounds, but I raised it on my shoulder and carried it like it was nothing. The older man was surprised and grateful. He offered to pay me, but I refused. Instead, I kissed him on his cheek, wished him a good day, and turned to leave. That's when it happened.

I'll never forget the moment our eyes met. Those amber pools called to me, begging me to get lost in them. This had to be Kyro. He was gorgeous. I had to keep reminding myself that we needed to keep to the quest. No matter how distracting his ebony curls or those broad shoulders covered in muscles that accentuated his olive skin were, I had to focus. Even his name was beautiful—Kyro. He was the first son of a god I had ever met. It was a little unnerving. He was so humble and so genuine. I had no expectations for this meeting since Ian hadn't even told me if Kyro was a person or a place. I felt as though I couldn't catch my breath, and my knees felt weak. At that moment, I could picture us in an embrace, about to kiss, my fingers tangled in his curls. Suddenly his thoughts were in my head; I could hear his initial impression of me.

She's incredible; I've never seen anything like her before. Her skin is so pale, with just a whisper of blue. Her hair is the color of midnight, the darkest shade I'd ever seen. Her physical strength caught me off guard as well. I wasn't prepared for someone half my size to be as strong as I am. How is she this strong? What is she? Can I trust her? Will she trust me?

And cue total embarrassment. I'm sure the combination of my initial thoughts, his thoughts, and the realization that I had heard them caused my cheeks to light up like a fire. What kind of charm had this demigod cast on me?

"Hello, are you Kyro? I was told you would be able to help me." I desperately wanted him to be Kyro, and I was confident it was he, but I needed to hear him say it for some reason.

"Yes, I'm Kyro. I've been expecting you. My father's seer told me of your visit many moon cycles ago, and I've been waiting."

Oh, I guess this part was going to be easier than I expected. At least I didn't have to convince him that I'm not crazy. And it sounded like he wanted to help. He held out his hand to shake mine. He smelled of the sea; it was an enchanting smell that I had never experienced.

"Would you like to join me on my boat, Sea Shadow, and we can discuss this matter further?" He smiled, showing slight dimples in his cheeks.

Again, I blushed. "I think that would be lovely. Thank you."

I took his hand and climbed on board the boat. Just as he let go, my foot slipped, and I started to fall. Kyro grabbed me, and the next thing I knew, I was staring into his amber eyes.

"Are you OK?" He asked, glancing at my lips. I blushed again. It would be so easy to lean forward and touch my lips to his. I swallowed hard, getting control of my thoughts.

"I'm fine, thank you. I slipped, that's all."

He gestured toward a door, and I knew that I would follow him anywhere if he asked. We ended up in the galley.

"You must be hungry after your journey from space. Let me get you something to eat and drink. Then we can discuss the quest."

"Thank you. It seems as though you may know more about it than I do, though."

He brought back two rolls and cups of ale. Most of what we had to eat on Calliope was freeze-dried or dehydrated and reconstituted, so fresh bread was a real treat. We sat there, eating for a moment before either of us spoke. It was unnerving how he would entirely focus on me, as though nothing else in the world existed but the two of us. As intimidating as it was, I liked it. Could I be interested in him? Was he interested in me? I needed to pull myself back and focus on the mission. I just couldn't escape the thoughts of being in his arms.

"I'm not sure where to begin. Do you want to tell me what you know, and then I can fill in what Ian has told me?" I wasn't even sure at this point if he knew about Ian.

He nodded. "I think that would be best. My father's seer has connected with your seer—I think you called him Ian?"

I nodded as he continued. "They have communicated a few times, so she knows what he desires to find and why. We aren't sure where to find it, but we know that he wants us to hunt down a magical dodecahedron. Father has permitted me to assist you on this quest. But I'm not sure what help they think I will be to you. My powers are limited, and it seems as though yours are as well."

I was instantly shocked. "But I... I don't...have powers."

"Of course, you do. You just haven't tapped into your powers yet. Ask your seer about it. Make him explain why he chose you for this quest. If you don't want to wait for your powers to surface, we could talk to Father and see if he would let you meet his seer. She may be able to help. In the meantime, I'll show you your room." As he spoke, Kyro escorted me to what would be my cabin on his boat.

When we arrived at the door, I responded, "I'll check with Ian and let you know. But I'm sure if I had powers, I would know." Before he could respond, I went inside and closed the door. I needed to have an earnest talk with a book.

I pulled the book out of my bag, sat on the bed, and began to flip through the pages. "Ian, why did you choose me for this? Kyro thinks I have magical powers, but I don't. I would know by now if I did, right? Please just tell me what's going on here." I then watched as the pages started to light up with that now-familiar glow.

Zoey, I told you, I had a vision of you being the savior. I'm not sure what else you want to know or even what more I could say to you at this point.

"Do I have magical powers that I don't know about?"

Oh, that. I was hoping we could avoid that for a while. I didn't want to be the one to tell you. As ironic as it sounds, given the current situation, I usually do try not to interfere by telling others about things I've seen in visions. But you've trusted me this far, so I will tell you. Yes, you do. But that's all I will say about it. You'll discover them at the moments when you need them. I have seen it. You will have what you need at the moment you need it to locate the dodecahedron and complete this quest.

"I'm just supposed to go along with all this, not knowing what's going to happen to me? You can't tell me what power or powers I have?"

Not at this moment. All I can tell you is that Kyro needs to sail south across the Mediterranean Sea. He will know where to stop. Once you get there, you must locate the cavern and search it for the dodecahedron or clues to where it is located. The cavern has information for your next step in the mission. I just don't know what you'll find there.

"I would like a decent night's rest first before we go sailing off to some uncharted island to search for some unknown cave for your missing magical trinket. Goodnight, Ian." With that, I slammed the book shut and shoved it back in my bag. I wasn't sure why I was so angry with him, but I felt like Ian could have told me more about my powers. I woke this morning thinking I was perfectly normal and then find out I have mysterious powers that will show themselves at random times. It was a lot to take in. And I was not a fan of keeping secrets, especially if they could be the difference between life and death. I put my bag on the floor and fell into the bed, asleep just as my head hit the pillow.

Little did I know, Kyro already knew we were to sail south and had begun preparations for our trip as I slept. He gathered supplies in town, loaded the boat, and had already cast off when I woke in the morning. I awoke to the rocking of the ship on the open sea and was startled. I rushed up on deck to find Kyro adjusting ropes on the sails to catch better gusts of wind.

"We should be there in a few days. You should eat some-thing." It seemed like he was always trying to feed me, which reminded me of being home with my parents. Sometimes the oddest things made a person feel at home in a new place.

"Thank you. Have you eaten?" I secretly hoped he had wait-ed for me, but I didn't know how long he had been up. I wanted to get to know him before we went too far into this quest. I had to be sure I could trust him, even though I felt like I could trust him with my life from the moment we met.

"I had breakfast before sunrise, but I could use a snack, and I'm sure you could do with some company. Am I right?"

"Definitely. And we can discuss the plan for this mission. Lead the way."

He led me back down to the galley, where he prepared breakfast for me and a snack for himself.

We talked about everyday things—what I studied in school, what it was like for him growing up on the sea—before we got into mission details.

"When we get to the island, the cavern will be on the west side of it. We can enter from that side and inspect the area." It seemed as though there was nothing to discuss; Kyro had it all planned out.

"What made you decide to help me?"

"What do you mean?" He sounded caught off guard at the question.

"I mean, I just showed up out of nowhere. You don't know me. Why would you decide to help me with this? Especially since Ian thinks it's going to be dangerous. How can you be so sure that you can trust me?"

"Father said it was to be my quest. His seer envisioned it, and thus it is. My destiny is entwined with yours. I think it's easier when you've dealt with fate your entire life. Let's eat and not worry about this right now."

We finished eating in silence. We had a couple more days to spend getting over the awkwardness of being thrust together on a mission to save the world. There was no point in trying to sort through everything at once.

The following two days passed, with Kyro checking the sails, making sure I ate, and telling me stories of sailing the open seas. In exchange, I shared stories I had read while on Calliope: fairy tales, histories, fiction. It seemed as though we would get along just fine, and my nerves faded over time. He told me a bit about his mother but never mentioned his father other than to discuss the seer who had given him this quest. I told him a bit about how I ended up moving to Calliope and what it was like growing up on the space station.

When we approached the island, it was just as he had said. The entrance to the cavern was visible from the shoreline. We carefully docked the boat far enough to be hidden from view and then headed toward the chamber entrance.

seventeen

Zoey

KYRO AND I CREPT slowly into the chamber. It was pitch black but for the glow of his amulet, and moisture hung in the air like a curtain. I wasn't sure what we would find in this cavern, but I was convinced it wouldn't be the dodeca. The best I could hope for was another clue to guide us along our journey. Given the sparks between Kyro and myself, I preferred it that way. I wanted an excuse to spend more time with him and get to know everything about him. As my thoughts were occupied, I lost my footing on the slick terrain. I would have fallen on my face if he hadn't acted so quickly. I swear he had the reflexes of a cat.

I suddenly found myself upright and spun around, nose to nose with him; his strong arms wrapped protectively around my waist. For one fleeting moment, I leaned in, our lips almost touching. Suddenly his amulet started to glow brighter, and we jumped apart. We were being urged further toward the chamber's center by the intensifying light emanating from the charm. There was a faint torchlight on the north wall of the room. We had entered from the west, so there was no light to our right. There was, however, a stone podium on the south wall, almost masked in darkness. We made our way over to it as stealthily as we could. There was no telling what kind of traps or challenges we could encounter. It was difficult to see in the sudden darkness as Kyro closed his hand over the amulet to mask our movements.

We reached the stone podium and inspected it for clues. It was so dark in that corner that we couldn't tell if there were clues or not. Kyro slowly opened his hand to allow some light from his amulet to escape. I saw papers on the podium crumpled and showed signs of water damage while they were currently dry. The documents contained sigils and runes, but I couldn't translate them without pulling out books from my bag. Since I knew we didn't have time for that, I carefully put all the papers inside one of the blank notebooks in my bag. We kept searching for anything that looked like it might help us find the dodeca.

I sensed our company before I saw them. My face must have alerted Kyro because he tensed up before I could say anything. Upon turning around, we were faced with the most terrifying thing I have ever seen. I don't even have words to describe them except to say that they looked like giant spiders. One was roughly six feet tall, while the other was somewhat smaller, closer to five feet tall. Their leg span seemed to be close to eight feet across. They seemed to be communicating in their own language and were moving around the chamber as if they were looking for something. I watched in horror as these creatures made their way closer to us, their mandibles working as though they were having a casual conversation, but the sounds they made weren't any language I had ever heard.

I let out a terrified gasp at the sight of them, and Kyro immediately clamped his hand over my mouth, pulling me back against him as he pressed against the wall in the darkness. I had a feeling we wouldn't get away as quickly as we had planned.

The spiders must have heard me because they turned and headed toward where we were hiding in the dark. Fortunately, they weren't armed. Unfortunately, neither were we. I had trained with Jack on Calliope, but that mainly was self-defense, and I wasn't sure if it would be enough to fend off an attack of this magnitude. I had no idea if Kyro was able to defend himself either. In retrospect, these are the things I should have considered before agreeing to this mission. There wasn't much time to berate myself for it, though, as our spidery friends spotted us at that moment.

The enormous spider started shooting a web at us in an attempt to capture us. All I could think was, how did these spiders get so big? Were all spiders on Earth this large? From the look on Kyro's face, I didn't think this was the case. Was this a science experiment gone wrong? If so, who had the capability of creating these monsters? Or did someone create giant spiders on purpose to kill anyone who entered the cave? I couldn't let that happen to us. I had to make sure Kyro was safe. We had to complete Ian's mission and save the world from what it had become. As I entertained these thoughts, Kyro attacked the smaller spider, who was coming at us quickly. He swept its legs right out from under it, knocking the monster on its back. I decided to try to subdue the enormous spider before it could web us. I wasn't sure what to do. I was terrified but started throwing pebbles at it to make it chase me until I had it under a stalactite. I picked up a rock about the size of my head and threw it at the stalactite, hoping to make contact. Not only did it make contact, but the stalactite fell on the giant spider, splattering his insides across me and the walls. Kyro was still hand-to-hand battling the smaller spider when the ceiling started to shake from the impact of the rock I threw. Stalactites began to fall all around us. He managed to maneuver the spider under one as it was falling, and before too much time had passed, that monster was a pile of guts as well. We hustled out as quickly as possible to avoid more monsters and falling rocks.

Kyro led me back to his boat. We boarded and headed back to his dock. The plan was to rest, eat, and then try to decipher the pages we found. Hopefully, there was something in them that would lead us to the location of the dodeca, or at least help us figure out who had it. I wanted to start studying immediately, but Kyro insisted that I at least take a few minutes to meditate if I wouldn't sleep. He made a valid point that if Ian could not locate the dodeca by scrying, these pages probably weren't a detailed map to its location. I decided to get some fresh air, then maybe lay down for a while.

EIGHTEEN

Ian

ONCE I HAD CONVINCED Zoey to take the quest, the real work began. I had to track down each element needed for the spell to reverse the first one. There were so many emails, text messages, and phone calls; I didn't think I'd ever find what I was looking for. I just had to be very careful of the spell's intent, or it wouldn't work the way I intended. I was planning to set things right, but I wasn't going to give any of my magic up to do it.

I felt terrible that I hadn't been candid with Zoey or her friends, but there was no way any of them would help if they knew the complete truth. I needed to beat the Order so I could take over. I had grand plans to make the world better. I just needed more power to do it. I knew I had to be careful of what I wrote in the book, and I needed to make sure there was no way someone could take the journal from Zoey by force. That would be priority one.

I made a list of the supplies I would need and the places they could be found. Since I couldn't leave my house anymore, I had to send for a delivery service. There was only one I trusted. I pulled out my cell phone and sent a text to MRU—I know, Magic-R-Us, it sounds ridiculous. I didn't choose the name, it just happens to be the best place for almost any magical supply, and they deliver. I got the response text and sent my list. The delivery person would do the rest, and I would have it within about three days.

As for why I couldn't leave my home, that was another story altogether. It wasn't so much that I couldn't leave at all as it was that the Order was hunting me, and my home was the only place that was warded, with protection spells, well enough to hide me. It was the one place they couldn't find, though my name was on the mailbox. I had paid dearly for the assistance in placing those wards. I still needed more resources, and these were the ones that couldn't be delivered. I cast a protective circle, then opened a portal into the library. It was a risky move, mainly since the library I chose belonged to the Order.

It was the one place where these specific tomes could be found together. Just as I suspected, they didn't even notice. I located the books I was looking for as quickly as possible and headed back through the portal without incident.

Once safely back at home, I closed the portal and got to work. It was going to be a long night of reading and spell crafting. Especially if the questers returned with the dodeca, then I would have another problem to deal with: activating it and figuring out precisely what it does.

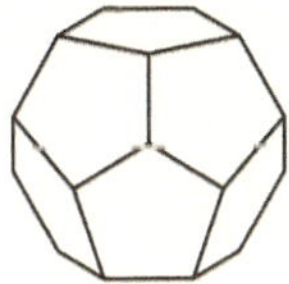

I wasn't sure how long I had been asleep, but I woke to pounding on the front door. I lifted my head from the book that had been my pillow, rubbed my eyes, and headed for the door. There was no way I was going just to open it, though. I looked out the peephole and spied the familiar red and yellow uniform. I opened the door quickly and pulled the kid inside. "You're just a child! Why did they send you?" The young girl looked up at me, eyes wide, and grinned. "I'm the only one who would deliver what you requested, sir. The others were too scared." She was just under five feet tall, with long dark red hair pulled into a braid that cascaded down her back. Her skin was tanned, and her golden eyes danced with mischief.

She removed a backpack and started digging inside. She named each item as she handed me each ingredient that had been on my list. Then with a triumphant smile, she said, "That's everything. And in record time. It only took me a day to get it all. Make sure you tell the Boss that, would ya?"

I checked off each item as it was handed to me. Some of it should have taken at least a day and a half to obtain, yet here this child was, almost two days early. "How did you do this so fast?" I had to know, though; I figured it had to be a power she had.

"If I told you that, you'd get me fired. Just be happy I got the stuff for you, and let the boss man know I did well. OK?"

This one had spunk. "What's your name, child?" I'd make sure to ask for her from now on when I needed deliveries.

"The name's Bailey, but my friends call me Bay. If you're tipping, we can be friends." I handed her an extra $20 bill on top of the cost of the shipment. "Yeah, mister, you can call me Bay. Who are you anyway? Why is everyone so scared to come to your house? And what are you doing with all this stuff? Some of it's pretty rare."

"That, my dear Bay, is an excellent question. Let's just be satisfied that they are, and you aren't, OK? That means more tip money for you, right? Does it matter the why of it or what I'm doing with it? As for who I am, my friends call me Ian. I think you and I can be friends, don't you?"

Her eyes were still wide from the large tip, and she nodded. "Just let us know when you need anything else, Ian. I'll be happy to deliver anytime." She closed the door behind her as she left.

I conjured up a basket to load my ingredients into and then headed back to the office with my haul. I needed to get everything organized and be ready when Zoey contacted me for her next step.

NINETEEN

Zoey

As I STOOD THERE on the deck of Kyro's ship, sailing across the murky waters, the breeze touching my face, I came to a realization. The world isn't as black and white as I had previously thought. To champion this quest, I would have to lean into the gray and trust that I would only do what was necessary to survive. Could I manage this without losing myself in the process? I wasn't proud of what I had to do in the cavern, but I knew it was them or me. There was no way around it. I had killed. Not with my hands, though it may yet come to that. Yes, it was self-defense, but it was still death. I wasn't sure I could wrap my head around that. I struggled with the moral dilemma that this quest may continue to force me into. Though I was relieved the spiders were dead instead of us, it still pained me to have been the cause of their demise.

As I tried to reconcile this new part of me with the old, I didn't hear Kyro come up behind me. He seemed to be already able to read me like a book. I wondered if that was the empath powers or if we honestly had a soul connection. I knew if I fell for him, I would never be the same. It didn't matter either way; time would tell—I just needed to let it play out however fate intended. He slipped an arm around my shoulders, and I leaned my head against his chest. I couldn't help but compare this with the last time I had seen Race. Those feelings didn't even come close to this. I tilted my head to look up at him, and he gently pressed his lips to my forehead.

"Are you OK?" he asked softly.

"What were those things?" I asked in response.

"I can honestly say that I have never seen anything like that in my life. I have no idea how those spiders got that big. It had to be magic or genetic engineering." His reply wasn't the answer I had hoped for, and I guess my face gave that feeling away. Kyro surprised me by taking my face in his hands.

"It's ok to mourn. You gave up your innocence to save our lives. I fear we will have to do more of this to survive. I just wanted to make sure you know you aren't alone. I'm here for you. If you want to talk, we can. Or if you just want to watch the ocean for a while, I'll be here with you. Unless you'd rather have some solitary time to process what happened?" His words were kind, and I could see the genuine concern in his eyes as he looked at me hopefully.

"Please stay with me. I was feeling so alone and distraught just before you came out here. Your touch is so comforting. Thank you...for everything. Just...hold me for a little while, please?"

With that, he put both arms around me and pulled me into him. I rested my cheek on his chest, and he put his cheek against my hair. At that moment, I remembered what had happened when we met. I marveled at the thoughts he had of me. I had never considered myself to be beautiful, or not for that matter. I had never given it much thought. I was aware that most people were attracted to members of the same race who look similar. While I was wrapped up in his arms, I was so glad this man was not one of those people. Just being with him made me feel so safe. I knew there was more danger in our future, but for this fleeting moment, I stood there, being held and watching the ocean.

As I listened to his heartbeat, I relaxed more and more. I was more tired than I was willing to admit. Kyro caught me dozing off while we were wrapped up together. He scooped me up and carried me down below to the cabins. I don't think I had ever trusted anyone this quickly before. Somehow I knew I had nothing to fear from him. He gently tucked me into my bed, kissed my forehead, and gently closed the door as he left. Less than a month into our journey, and I already knew I'd lost my heart. I just hoped that was all I lost on this journey.

I was so relaxed when Kyro left that I thought I was asleep, or I may have been. Then suddenly, everything around me changed, and I was in a dark chamber. I looked around, confused. There were two candles on either side of the room, but it was primarily shadows. I looked down at myself and realized I must be dreaming. I was wearing a navy blue ball gown, the exact shade of my hair. When I lifted my eyes from the dress, they met with someone staring at me. He was tall, with blond hair shaved on the right side, and the left hung over his eye. The eye that wasn't covered was blue, lit with desire. He gave me a crooked smile and held a hand out as if to ask me to dance. I didn't see any reason to refuse; after all, it was only a dream, right?

He slipped his arms around me, and we twirled to soft music. As we danced, I heard a voice in my head. It was dark and felt sinister. "This could be your life, my dear, nothing but peace, beauty, and music. Anything you dream of could be yours. All you have to do is give me the book."

I looked at my dance partner, who was focused on the music. "Did you hear that?" He looked at me, raised an eyebrow, and shrugged. This guy wasn't going to be any help, so I tried to break free of his hold, but I couldn't. I couldn't make my arms move from around his neck. It was as if I was frozen there, stuck in that dance. I started to scream, trying to wake myself from what was turning into a nightmare.

The voice came back, angrier this time. "You cannot escape me, girl. I will have the book. And you, if I decide, that's what I want. You won't stop me." At this point, I was terrified and started praying to wake up. "You think this is a dream? Ha! I've taken you, silly girl. I've proven that I will win by stealing you in your sleep. I can keep you here forever if I want." As if to prove his point, the beautiful man holding me changed before my eyes. His hair turned gray, his skin ashen as if he had aged instantly. He now appeared to be well over ninety, whereas before, he looked to be my age.

His face turned to me, and he finally spoke. "Why fight? You can stay here with me. Don't you want to be with me?" While the words escaped his lips, he began to crumble and turn to dust in my arms. It was horrifying. Tears streamed down my face, and I kept screaming over and over. I needed to find a way out of here.

The candlelight was just enough to make out a door on the south wall. I started running toward it as the floor seemed to turn to mud. My feet began sinking with each step. I was in a complete panic before I made it halfway to the door. "Calm down, Zoey, you can do this." I knew it was silly, but talking to myself helped. I was able to keep it together long enough to maneuver the steps to reach the door. As soon as my hand touched the knob, the room disappeared, and I was in a forest, with fog so thick I couldn't see my hand in front of my face. I chose a direction and started to run. I had to watch my feet and what was in front of me carefully to avoid falling or running into a tree. When I thought I was careful, I tripped over a root and face-planted into the trunk of a small tree.

I sat down and rubbed my hands over my face—that hurt. I'd never had a dream hurt before. Maybe the voice was telling the truth. Had I been captured? Where was I? Would Kyro come for me? I pulled my hands from my face, and there was blood on one. Even better, my face was or cut, and I was bleeding. At least it wasn't that bad, just a little bit of blood. I pulled every ounce of inner strength I had and forced myself to my feet. I would not let this bad guy win. I didn't even know who was after me or why. I vowed that I would discover who was trying to capture me and why before I gave up.

I started walking through the trees, making sure to go slowly and watch my feet more closely. Suddenly there was a clearing in front of me, with a circle of stones in the middle. The sun was shining on the center of the ring, and clouds were forming around it. I could feel the power oozing from the circle and desperately wanted to get there. I scanned the area to make sure it was safe to continue. I didn't see anything, so I moved forward. Lightning struck the ground next to my barefoot, just missing the hem of my dress.

I jumped and let out a squeal. Then I ran as fast as I could toward the center of the circle. I hoped I was right, and that would be my way out of this place. I didn't think I'd be finding out any time soon, though. As soon as I crossed into the circle, I fainted and hit the ground. Everything went hazy. I couldn't see, hear, or move. It was the most terrifying thing that had happened to me yet.

I don't know how long I was like that before I came to. It was dark, and I wasn't sure where I was. I was lying down, so I sat up and looked around. I saw a glow coming from the floor across the room. That must be a door. I crawled out of the bed that I was in and crept to the door. I tested the handle, and it wasn't locked. The door opened, and I could see from the light in the hall that I was on Kyro's boat again.

I turned the light on, closed the door, and strolled back to the bed. I sat there with my back against the headboard, shivering, convinced I'd never sleep again. I ran my hands over my face, and when there were traces of blood on my finger-tips, I knew that everything that eerie voice had told me was right. I wrapped the blanket tightly around me and stared at the door as if something was coming to get me. It may have been, after what I had just experienced. At some point, sleep retook me, but it was uneasy and dreamless.

When I finally woke, I was still on edge. I gathered the books I needed to decipher the pages we found and headed to the galley. I needed some tea to calm my nerves. More than that, I needed answers.

twenty

Kyro

IT HAD BEEN A long, eventful day, and I knew sleep wouldn't come quickly. I needed answers, and there was only one person who could give them to me. I headed back to my room to get the supplies I would need and then went back up to the deck. I wanted to do this under the stars.

I decided to consult with my father's seer once Zoey was tucked into bed and asleep. I knew she would have some answers for me about Zoey and what was to come. Using the powers my father had granted me, I summoned Ariella in a scrying bowl under the moonlight.

"Kyro, is everything OK? How can I help?" It seemed strange for an all-knowing being to ask if everything was OK, but I knew that her powers didn't allow her to see everything all the time.

"Ari, can you give me some insight?" I had to word my questions carefully, or I wouldn't get answers. I had worked with Ari before. She was a stickler for protocol.

"Kyro, my dear boy, you know I cannot reveal all. I can try to answer your questions if you'd like." That answer was disappointing but expected.

"Thank you, Ari. I need to know why I was selected for this mission. And what is with Zoey? She has powers but doesn't know what they are or how to discover them. How can I help her?" I didn't expect her to answer most of my questions, but I felt like they had to be asked. Even if she didn't answer, maybe she would point me in the right direction.

"Ah, Kyro, you must be patient with her. She will discover her powers as they are needed. And she will need you to help her learn to control it. She is a mighty being, even if she doesn't seem so. Her powers will be dangerous and wild and will need to be tamed for your safety. As for why you were selected to help, that I cannot say. I had a vision of the sorcerer Ian, and when we spoke, I knew it was you that he needed. After discussing it with your father, he agreed that you should be allowed to go on this quest. Are you regretting your decision?"

"No, Ari, not at all. But I'm feeling pulled to her, and I can't figure out exactly why. Can you help me with that?" I was hopeful that she would give me some answers instead of talking in circles like she was known to do.

"Well, I have seen things...that may indicate she is of importance to you...I cannot say for sure, because you do have a choice in the matter...but she may be the mate to your soul. You can choose to act on this or to fight against it. But I see it will end the same either way. And I will not tell you the ending, so do not ask."

"The mate to my soul? Like my soulmate? As in forever? And you weren't going to tell me? This is huge. If this is true, and we're fated to be together, I have to go on with this mission. I will have to protect her and make sure this mission doesn't fail. Thank you, Ari."

With that, her image faded away, and I was alone on the deck once more. I had much to consider and wondered if any of it had ever been in my hands at all. I decided to go for a swim to clear my head. Most people would have been terrified to jump into the ocean in the middle of the night. A son of the sea was not one of them. I loved the water, and it was just what I needed to clear my head. After my swim, I climbed back on the boat and retired to my room.

I sorted through my books and laid out the ones I thought would help figure out the symbols and runes we discovered, and then I got ready and went to sleep.

When I awoke, I gathered the books I had laid out and took them to the galley, where I found Zoey waiting with the papers. Her books were strewn across the table, and she had already begun to decipher the pages. Zoey looked exhausted like she hadn't slept. Given that she appeared to be sleeping peacefully when I left her, it concerned me.

"Hey, are you alright?" I spoke softly, trying to avoid startling her.

She jumped anyway. "Oh, Kyro. I'm sorry, you scared me. I was working on the pages." Her eyes darted toward the door as though she was watching for something.

I could see that her lip was busted, and there were dark circles under her eyes. "What happened?" I could tell she didn't want to talk about it, and much as I wanted to push, I knew it wasn't the time. She shook her head a little, then went back to the page she was working on.

"It's OK. You're safe now, and if you want to talk about it, I'm here. Ok?" She nodded and gave me a small smile. I was worried but knew when she was ready, we would talk about it.

We sorted and sifted through information for a few hours before we found anything of use. After a few more hours, Zoey had a breakthrough and figured out what the pages said. We had our next clue and knew what the next step had to be. It was inspiring to watch her work, seeing her face scrunched in concentration and then watching her eyes light up when she figured it out. I would have known my heart was in danger, even without Ari's warning.

twenty-one

Zoey

Once we deciphered the symbols that we found at the spider lair, we headed west to Spain. According to the pages we translated, there was a fire wizard in Spain who may help us. Of course, the pages' existence with this information meant someone else was looking for this wizard as well. We had to act quickly. Ian was convinced that this fire wizard who simply went by the name Q was a direct descendant of his friend Ed, who had been given the power to create and control fire when the change occurred. It didn't matter to me if they were related or not—I just had to convince this Q that we were worth helping. We spent the next few days sailing toward Spain as though we were simply tourists heading on an adventure, with no care in the world.

We docked the boat at one of the busiest ports shortly after breakfast and ventured carefully into the city to find Q. Kyro spoke fluent Spanish and was able to talk to some locals. He casually mentioned that his friend, Q, lived in Spain, but he couldn't remember where. We found someone who knew of Q, pointed us to a town inland, and a few hours' walk from where we docked. We gathered supplies from the local street vendors and headed north.

It was a three-hour walk, and by the time we got to Bella Agua, we were more than ready for lunch and a rest. But there would be time for both once we found Q. Kyro spotted the local inn a few blocks ahead of us. We figured that might be the best place to start our search.

As we walked in, I looked around, amazed at the architecture and the clientele. I still hadn't adjusted to how different things were here on Earth than life on the space station. Everything on Calliope had been within walking distance, and nothing was decorated as boldly as this place. There were humanoids and aliens alike in the lobby. Some were waiting for rooms, others were just hanging out, and still, others were there to work. A handful of the people in the lobby were wearing outfits that left very little to the imagination. Glancing around the room,

I noticed a woman sitting at the bar who was only wearing a bra and panties.

"Kyro, isn't that strange?" I kept my voice low and pointed as inconspicuously as I could. His eyes followed my gesture, and he let out a soft laugh.

He pulled me close and whispered his answer in my ear. I had been protected from some of the seedier aspects of life on Earth and could not recognize a prostitute when I saw one. Lucky for me, the ones at this inn had already been spoken for and didn't bother with me. I had thought their fashion choices were a bit strange, and that was what led me to ask about it.

We walked up to the front desk. The guy handling the desk was thin, with gray hair that came down just past his ears and pale skin from spending too much time indoors. He looked to be human, but it was so hard to tell with all the different species in the area. He looked up at us from the chair he was sitting in, with kind eyes and a warm smile. "Hello there. I'm Gerald. How may I help you folks today?"

"We're looking for a friend of ours. Maybe you can point us in the right direction. Do you know Q?" I hoped that Kyro was a good liar; otherwise, I didn't think Gerald would be much help to us.

"Oh, everyone in town knows Q. But I'm not sure I believe that you know Q. What business do you have here?" Of course, he didn't believe us. Now what?

"OK, I'll level with you. I'm sorry. We've never met Q, but we were told to come here and ask for help. And that Q would be the best person for the job. Please, can you help us?" Good plan, Kyro; honesty is the best way to handle this situation. I silently prayed Gerald would help us.

"I'll send for Q, and we'll see what happens after you talk. Please find a seat in the lobby. It sounds like you may want to look for a somewhat private space. I'll let you know when Q gets here." He ran his hand over the stubble on his chin and then turned away to take care of our request.

"Thank you. We will look for a quiet spot, and we'll wait."

We walked away as he pulled a communicator out of his pocket and began typing away. I asked Kyro if he had one of those communicators because I hadn't seen him use one in the time we had spent together. "I spend all my time on the sea and have no use for a comm. But if you need one, I'm sure we can find one while we're in town."

"I'm relieved you don't have one. I didn't exactly leave home on the best terms, and it's better if they can't use it to track me down."

"I understand. It can't be easy for you to be away from home like this. Are you homesick for space and your family?"

Before I could answer, a six-foot-tall, muscular yet slender half-elven woman with long red hair cascading down her back walked in the door and headed straight for us. Our eyes met, and instantly, I knew this was Q. Why had Ian not told us Q was a woman?

"You the ones who came looking for me?" She was direct and blunt, two charming qualities, given where I came from.

"We are," I responded, "We've come to ask for your help. Please let us explain."

"Fine, but not here. This place is not secure—the Order watches. Come with me. Then I'll hear you out and decide if I'll let you live."

Kyro didn't seem fazed by that statement, but I was utterly taken aback. Did I hear that correctly? Did she just threaten us? Lucky for me, Kyro took charge to cover my reaction.

"Very well, lead the way," Kyro spoke as he gently grabbed my arm to lead me out the door. "We're going to convince her to help us, right?" He winked at me; I blushed and then nodded.

This treatment was somewhat surreal. I took from the look Q gave me when she first saw me that we had a mutual connection. I may have been wrong.

We followed her out the door and down the street. She turned left at an intersection and then ducked down an alleyway. We followed close behind, moving quickly enough that it was difficult to keep track of how many turns we had taken. At the end of the next alley was a wall; we'd hit a dead-end—not literally, I hoped.

"Did you notice anyone following us?" Q asked anxiously. She hadn't spoken until this moment.

"Yes, but we lost him a couple of blocks back." I wasn't even sure how I knew we had been followed, but I was sure the gentleman in the bowler hat and blue suit had been trying to keep up with us.

"Good. I just had to know if you noticed him. That guy gives me the creeps," Q stated, "and he's a member of the Order, so that's even more reason to avoid being caught by him."

She drew a sigil on the wall with her finger, and a door appeared out of thin air. Q opened it and motioned us inside. We quickly crossed the threshold, and the door disappeared behind Q.

"That's better. Now we're in a secure location. This is my base of operations. Thank you for trusting me. I know Gerald wouldn't have let me get caught, but he may not have been able to save the two of you. Easier to avoid those situations than to fight, especially in public. Don't get me wrong, I love to fight, and I always win, mostly because I choose when and where I do it. Now...tell me your story."

We followed her into a drawing room and sat on couches positioned around the fireplace. The room was a pale blue and reminded me of the boat's calming view as we sailed. She gestured to the hot cider that appeared on the table as she waved her hand, and we settled in to tell her why we had come.

Once we finished, she nodded, and it was her turn. Q explained that her given name was Quinn, and she was indeed a descendant of Ian's friend Ed, though she never knew him. He had lived to the age of 200 years old and died of old age, unlike most of his friends. She didn't tell us much, but what information she gave was enough to know we would need her help.

When it was all said and done, she agreed to come with us and assist with the quest to set the world right. But only after a good night's sleep. We would head back to the boat in the morning. She led us to a guest bedroom, assuming that Kyro and I were together and would want to share a room. Neither Kyro nor I corrected her. We stepped inside and said our "goodnights" to our hostess, and he closed the door.

"If this makes you uncomfortable, I can sleep on the floor," Kyro said as he gestured to the singular double bed in the center of the far wall.

"I... uh...well," I was seriously dumbfounded. Was Kyro asking me to have sex with him? I was familiar with the ritual; I just typically wanted to know someone more than a few days first. I know it had been a few weeks by now, but still, that's not much time. I mean, Race and I had been intimate, but that was after I had known him for years.

"I don't want you to be uncomfortable. The floor doesn't look very soft."

"We can sleep next to each other, then...I promise to b
ehave...unless you have other ideas?" His eyes gleamed with
mischief. I think he was enjoying my embarrassment.

"Sleep will be fine. Why didn't you tell Q that we aren't
together like that? What other ideas do you think I have?" I
knew I was talking too fast, but I was still somewhat shocked
at the turn this conversation was taking. I didn't want to seem
like a prude, but at the same time, I hadn't known him long
enough to be having the thoughts I had been having, and I
wasn't comfortable telling him about it.

"Well, how about I show you?" he said as he walked over to
me, "I, for one, have wanted to do this since the moment we
met." He wrapped his arms around my waist, pulling me close.
His lips were a whisper away from mine. He slid his hand up
my back, and I felt his fingers in my hair. He touched his lips
to mine, gently at first, and then passion took over. He wasn't
rough with me, but he didn't kiss me like I was fragile either.
His lips were soft but demanding, begging me for more, his
tongue teasing my lips apart to dance with his own. I wrapped
my arms around his shoulders and fisted my hands in his hair.
Our kiss lasted for a few moments more, but just when I started
to feel lightheaded, he pulled away.

"Do you have ideas now? And I guess I didn't tell her because I was glad she saw what we feel for each other. Even if
you aren't ready to admit it yet." How could he be teasing me
after kissing me like that?

"I..." I had no idea what to say to him. Everything that
popped into my head sounded completely stupid. He must
have been able to tell from my face that coherent thought was
not happening at that moment. I scrunched my face up as I
searched for words that made sense.

"I'm sorry, was that out of line? I was sure you wanted me to kiss you. Please forgive me." He sounded scared, like he was convinced he had upset me.

At least he was a gentleman. "I'm fine. There's nothing to apologize for. Yes, I've wanted to kiss you like that since the day we met as well. I just didn't realize you felt the same."

"I felt an instant connection to you when we met, Zoey. I think we're fated to be together. I just didn't, and don't, want to scare you off by moving too quickly." He rubbed a hand up and down my arm from my wrist to shoulder and back as he spoke.

"I felt it too. I need to focus on the quest—though. I can't lose sight of what needs to be done. I was chosen for a reason." I couldn't quite bring myself to meet his gaze. I knew looking into his eyes would be my downfall.

He tilted my chin up with his hand, so I had no choice but to look him in the eyes. "Does that mean you don't want to see what this is between us?" It was as if he knew I wouldn't be able to tell him "no" if our eyes locked.

"Of course I do. But I want to take it slowly. There's no need to rush, especially if we complete this quest and fix the world. Then we'll have the rest of our lives to discover what this is and if it's what we want." I didn't presume to know what he was thinking or that he would want to be with me for eternity. We had barely known each other for about a week at this point.

He leaned down and pressed his lips to mine again. This time I felt the heat of passion, but more restrained and sweeter. I could tell that he wanted me, but also that he cared enough not to push me.

"We should get some sleep," he said when he finally broke the contact between our lips. We walked over to the bed together and laid down together. "I just want to hold you, if that's OK?"

"I'd like that," I responded and laid my head on his chest. Within five minutes, I was sound asleep. For the first time in as long as I can remember, I didn't have my usual dream of being chased by demons.

I woke early the following day, anxious to get the journey started. Kyro's arms were still around me, so I settled back into him and tried to relax while I waited for him to wake up. A few minutes later, he began to stir. I turned my head and pressed my lips to his. He hummed and pulled me closer, intensifying the kiss. It felt like home; waking up next to him was as natural as breathing.

"Good morning, beautiful. How did you sleep?" He always seemed so considerate.

"I slept well. How about you?" I didn't want to tell him I was anxious to get Q and head out.

"Very well. But we should probably get moving, so we make it back to the boat before it's too late to sail out today." He already knew I was anxious. I just wasn't sure how.

"Good idea, let's find Q and get moving."

And with that, we got up and headed back to the drawing-room where we met last night. Q was waiting for us with a rather extensive breakfast.

"I trust you both slept well?" Q asked between bites of bacon.

Kyro and I nodded. Q gestured to the food, and we helped ourselves. After breakfast, Q showed us to the supply room. She explained there was a cart we could use to take any supplies we needed to the boat. We quickly inspected her inventory and chose items that we thought would come in handy. Food, weapons, blankets, clothing--she had everything. We packed the cart, hitched up her horses, and headed back to the docks.

When we arrived at Kyro's boat, someone was waiting for us. Kyro and I were hesitant, but Q walked right up to this mysterious stranger and grabbed him into a bear hug, picking him up off his feet.

"New friends, this is James. He is my favorite. He will take the horses and cart back to my place for us." James was a couple of inches shorter than Q, with strawberry blond hair and olive skin.

We greeted each other, and then James and Q walked away for a private conversation as Kyro and I loaded our wares onto the boat. Once she returned, we settled in for our trip. There were plenty of things on the ship that needed to be done, so Kyro delegated some jobs to us, and we all got to work. We would have a few days at least to figure out our next move.

twenty-two

q

When I had pulled James away from the others, I explained that I would be leaving to help them. Then I told James how they would help me, but they didn't know it yet. I had been trying to trap the Chairman for years, and with all the research I had done, I knew he was after the book. It wasn't by chance that I made them tell me everything before I decided if I would help or not. I had been trained by the best, and I wouldn't fail this mission. It had become my life's purpose.

"I'm concerned that you're getting in too deep. Can't you just let the specialty team handle the Chairman and the Order?"

"No, James, I can't. You know that. I need to be the one to take him down."

"But it's not your responsibility to fix the world. Don't you understand you're risking not only your life but also theirs by doing this?"

"Yeah, I am aware. Everything you've told me indicates that the Chairman wants this girl and the book she has. This is my chance; I have to do this now. I can draw him out and finally get him. I just have to get them to trust me first."

"And what about Mama Bear? You know she's not going to be happy about it when she finds out." Ouch, that was a low blow. James went from begging me to threatening me. I already knew our boss would be pissed that I took off after the Order by myself. She would think I needed a whole team, and better yet that I shouldn't be on the team at all. I knew she thought I was a loose cannon; I just didn't care what she thought. Not that I was eager to lose my position or my freedom. I was aware that following this lead could land me in jail or worse.

"Then you have to make sure she doesn't find out right away, that's all."

"And how do you propose I do that? I'm not going to lie to her. I'd rather not throw my career away the way you are. You know she'll have you fired and ruin your life for not following orders. Why can't you just follow protocol and ask her to send you?"

"You know as well as I do, James, that she wouldn't send me. She would send anyone but me because I'm not going to get emotionally attached to the puppets I use to get in. I won't hesitate to kill them all if they cross me. And she can't handle that. It'll be fine, I promise. Look, I just need you to let her know that I'll check in soon. And be very vague about where I'm going and what I'm doing. Ok?" James nodded in acceptance and then turned and walked away.

There were moments when I considered the choices that led me here and wondered how things would be different if I had taken the opposite path. Would we have gotten married, had kids, and settled down in a small town? I would never know now because I had decided not to go down that path. Of course, without my previous choices, I would never have met him in the first place. And that was one thing I would never regret. But the choice that led me away from him would always come into question, especially when I had to make another decision that could forever change my destiny. I had been chasing the Chairman for so long; I didn't know what else to do.

I knew that my obsession with the Order and the Chairman wasn't healthy, but honestly, what obsession was? I had always been cocky, but I didn't think that's what this was. I believed I was the best person for the job, and I wouldn't give up until I completed it. I spent the night before researching everything Kyro and Zoey had told me, as well as their backgrounds. I always knew everything I could about everyone I worked with, which is why James was my favorite. He was the best researcher I had ever met and was pretty handy where tech was concerned. If you had a secret, James would find it.

James' talent is how I knew about who Kyro was and what he was capable of. I had an entire file on him that I still had to read. I wasn't sure I could trust him yet, or her for that matter, though her backstory was less impressive than his. Being the son of a god had way more potential than the daughter of military parents. Of course, if my research was accurate, she had no clue who or what her parents were. I was planning not to be the one who told her about any of it. I was extremely surprised by our unexpected connection. I didn't want to be the one to say to her about that either.

I planned to bide my time with Kyro and Zoey until I discovered if they were trustworthy. I wondered if they had figured out that they were in love with each other. It only took five minutes of watching them both know. But it didn't appear that either of them had figured it out yet. Add that to the list of things I wasn't going to tell them. I hoped I could get my hands on the book long enough to see how it worked. I'd heard about it since training, and the whole story fascinated me. I had been told fairy tales as a child, but this was so much bigger than that. This book was our history, our lives, the reason everything in our world was the way it was. The man behind this book was responsible for all of it. He turned magic loose, and we knew he was trying to lock it back down. I just wanted to find out why. What reason could he have for wanting to take it away from those of us who were lucky enough to have it? I get that some people used magic for less than ethical purposes, but that didn't mean I should give my magic up. I was fighting to keep it.

I wondered if Zoey and Kyro had any idea who I worked for. I wasn't sure they would like it, so I decided to keep it to myself. There was no reason to put them in more danger than they already were. I needed to check in with HQ, but I couldn't do it in the open, so I had to have James send a message that I was going under. I would check in when I could. It would have to be today, though, or they'd come looking for me. I had no desire to be considered a deserter. The consequences for that were worse than anything the Order could do to me.

Once we got the supplies loaded and the boat was out on the open sea, I gave the excuse that I was worn out. Of course, Kyro insisted I retire to my room for the night to rest. It was the perfect cover, allowing me privacy to make my call. When I was sure the coast was clear, I set up the silence net and pulled out my comm device. I opened a secure connection and dialed the number that would connect me to Headquarters. Within a minute, the call was answered.

"Yes?" I knew that was the response I would get when I first thought about calling. It's also the reason I called the second in command instead of the boss.

"I know James told you everything. I'm on board the boat. With any luck, this will be who leads me to the Chairman. This could all be done soon." There was a chuckle from the other end of the line.

"It's cute how you think you can take on the Order by yourself. You're going to get yourself killed; you know that, right?"

It was the same fight we always had when I checked in. "I'll be fine. I finally have a real lead on him. I'm not giving up now. I can do this. Please trust me. Just stall her for a while, and give me a chance."

"OK, I trust you. I'll do my best to redirect her efforts, but you know how she is. If she gets wind of this, you'll be publicly tried and most likely locked up. Let us know if you need anything. We're always close by." The call was disconnected.

It was a good thing I had told the others I was worn out because I needed the time to plan out how I would handle this mission. And I was exhausted, so I climbed into my bed and let my mind play out possible scenarios until I fell asleep.

twenty-three

Kyro

After convincing Q to help us and then gather supplies and get the boat loaded, everyone went their separate ways to relax and settle in for the night. I waited until the others had gone to their rooms. I wanted to keep this ritual all to myself. I walked back up on the deck, took my shirt off, and dove into the water for my nightly swim. I hadn't been able to do it every night since Zoey came on board, and I had missed it. I had managed to sneak away a few times, but not often enough to quench the need in my soul.

I wasn't sure how I would explain to Zoey and Q who I was. I had wanted to tell them, but I could never be sure who I could trust. Some people wanted to either use me to gain favor with my father or use me to hurt him that it was hard to be honest about who he was. Even if we didn't see eye to eye about anything, he was still my father and my home ruler. He deserved my respect and whatever protection I could give.

I also hadn't decided if Q was trustworthy yet. I could tell she felt the same about us, but she seemed to have more information on us than we had on her. I would have to find a way to fix that. Perhaps my father would be able to help. I swam around the boat for a while by myself, and then I called out to Mateo. I knew I could talk to him, and he would help me figure out what Q was after.

I saw him swim up, and he had brought Isa and Ari with him. They had been my best friends for years, and when I was with my father, I spent most of my time with them. It was comforting to be in the company of my friends once more. It had been far too long since I had been to my father's home. I wanted to stay close to my mother when she was ill, and of course, my father understood. He loved her, even if he couldn't stay with her and be what she wanted. I knew that no matter what he said or did, he regretted leaving her.

I hadn't been the same since her death, and I knew he could sense it. That was part of the reason I hadn't been to see him. I didn't think I could take seeing the pain on his face. And with my powers, there was no way he could hide it from me. But that didn't matter right now. I would deal with my father at some point, but that was not an issue for today. Today, I would swim with my friends and try to forget.

I wasn't sure how I would ever explain to Zoey that the Order killed my mother. She deserved to know everything. I just wasn't sure I could tell her. How do you tell the girl you're falling in love with that your mother was a part of a secret organization bent on wiping magic from the Earth? How do you tell her that your mother wanted to get rid of you because of your powers?

At first, she had been convinced that by working with the Order, she could find a way to remove my powers without killing me. In the end, she seemed to have changed her mind about letting me live. We both knew if it was possible, it was going to hurt. If it hadn't been for my father, I would be a prisoner of the Order right now. I knew they did experiments on magical people, and it wasn't something I wanted to be a part of.

I tried hard to avoid thinking about her. Mack and Gill promised me that they would never tell anyone about her connection with the Order or her attempt to kill me. It wasn't something a mother should have done, but she was brainwashed by those psychos and had no idea what she was doing. It was almost as though her death was a mercy killing, as it freed her from the all-consuming need she had to lay waste to those of us with powers.

I missed her every day, but not who she was at the end. I missed who she was in the beginning. I missed the sweet, caring, nurturing woman my father had fallen in love with, even if it was only briefly. She loved him, and because of that, it broke her heart having me around after he broke things off with her. She grew to despise me because my father would spend time with me but refused to see her. I hated being in the middle, but it didn't matter because it wasn't long after the break up that she got involved with the Order.

In the beginning, she tried to pull me into it as well. With my powers, I was able to see the darkness taking hold of her. I left home and went off on my own and had lived on my boat ever since. I'll never forget that day, though, when Mack, Gill, and I were going to try to visit her and convince her to leave the Order. Just as we pulled the boat up to the dock, she came to the door, waved, and headed back inside. Less than a minute later, the entire house exploded. It was nothing but a shell in a matter of minutes.

The pain was all-consuming, and I was taken to my father. He locked me in my room, or so he called it, as I had never really lived there, just visited from time to time. I stayed in that room, allowing no visitors to come inside, until my step-mother, Amphi, forced her way in. She comforted me and stayed with me until I was ready to let the grief go and move on with my life.

My father and I had never been close, but I grew up loving his wife. After my mother's death, that love grew even more. She was the kindest, most loving woman I'd ever known. I visit with her frequently, even more than I see my father. I had asked her opinion on this quest before I accepted it because I valued her thoughts. She told me that there was a time in every man's life when he had to decide if he would chase destiny or let it come to him. I wasn't exactly sure what she had meant, but she seemed pleased when I decided to go.

Zoey

I wasn't sure why I woke in the middle of the night, but I felt like fresh sea air would make me relax, and I would want to sleep again. Plus, there was a chance that Kyro was awake as well, and I hoped that I would see him out there. We hadn't had a moment alone since we boarded the boat and set out to the south. Now reserved for ferrying the last of Earth's resources, the Suez Canal wasn't an option. Our new plan was to sail around Africa and head toward Japan, where Ian was convinced the next piece of the puzzle would be located. We had discussed our next move with him after Q got settled into her room. According to Kyro, he knew a place in Africa where we could stop for supplies and possibly more help.

It seemed as though the boat was moving slower than it had during the day, probably because the sails weren't open now. They were tied up, and the masts looked like skeletons in the darkness. There was faint moonlight illuminating the deck and the water around the vessel. I looked around but didn't see anyone else on the deck. I could swear that I felt Kyro nearby, but there was no one visible. I walked over to the edge, grabbed the railing, and looked up at the sky. There were stars as far as I could see. I understood why he was so drawn to the water. It was gorgeous here. I never wanted to leave. It was the most fantastic thing to see the stars from this angle compared to looking at them from space. I heard splashing below me just at the surface of the water. I peered over the edge and was astonished at what I saw.

Kyro, swimming in the ocean. Not just Kyro, though; he had friends—three to be exact. And a tail. It was blue like the ocean, with touches of silver and green. It indeed was a beautiful mermaid tail—merman tail? I wasn't sure what to call it. But a tail! What? I'm pretty sure he didn't have that earlier. I think I would have noticed him flopping around on deck with a tail! I gasped before I could stop myself, and they all turned. His friends were mermaids too, but I didn't know what to think about Kyro. I had never read about a mermaid or merman who had legs on land and a tail in the water. And I had read a lot of mythology, from many different regions, but nothing about anything like this.

One of his friends was female, with waist-length, wavy, russet-brown hair, skin the color of toasted almonds, and a tail the colors of the sunset...red, orange, yellow, with a multi-colored bra top to match. She was devastatingly beautiful. It was difficult to tell her eyes' exact color, but they were dark and seemed to dance when she smiled.

Another was a male who had well-tanned olive skin, with long, sandy-blonde hair and a tail with yellow and green shades. I remembered reading a book about surfing, and he looked just like that type of person. He looked to be about the same age as Kyro. He was more beautiful than the first mermaid if that was even possible. I mean, how can a man be beautiful? But he was. It seemed as though his eyes were lighter than the first female's, possibly blue or green.

The third one was the most striking of them all. She was female, her skin pale, so much so that it was impossible to tell what color it was, with dark hair—it was hard to know if it was black, or dark blue like mine, or perhaps a deep purple, even in the moonlight. Her tail was shades of pink and purple, blended beautifully, and she wore a strapless bikini top that matched as well. Her eyes seemed to be a medium color, not too dark, and not too light either. There was something magical about them; when they met mine, I felt an instant kinship with her. It was unlike anything I had ever experienced before.

The four of them together were a striking picture, like something from a mythology book I had read about mermaids and sirens, who could make people temporarily fall in love with them by simply looking into their eyes. I wondered if that was why I was so drawn to Kyro.

Before I could back away and run to my room, Kyro was standing next to me, on two legs, just as he had been when I met him. "What? How? I...I...I don't understand."

"Zoey, it's OK. I'm sorry, I should have told you. I know it's a shock. Please, will you let me explain? Come, sit over here with me in the moonlight."

I did as he asked because I totally trusted him and genuinely wanted to know how this was possible, even in my shock. He took my hand and guided me to the bench.

"I've told you that my father has a seer and that he sent me on this quest. His seer is Ariella— she's just there." He gestured to the third mermaid, the one who seemed to look into my soul. She raised her hand in a shy wave. "That's Mateo, and that's Isa." As he pointed, they gave me huge smiles and waved hello. "You know that my father is a god, but you never asked me which one. Would you like to know now?"

I didn't trust myself to speak, so I looked at him with tears in my eyes and nodded. I wasn't sure that I wanted to know, but I felt like I needed to.

"Good. OK, well, here goes. My father...is Poseidon, the god of the seas. He gave me a choice to be a merman or human. You see, my mother is human, and I visited her from time to time, but my home is the sea. I couldn't just abandon my mother. Father agreed that I should be able to visit her whenever I wanted. I learned to sail so I could be closer to home and still have some adventure. When I am in the ocean, or the sea...or any natural body of water, I can turn my legs into a tail. Most of my father's children either have legs or a tail. I got to have both, which is a rare and cherished gift. I hope this doesn't make you regret our kiss, and I truly hope you still want to be with me. Please, Zoey, say something?"

"I...I'm not sure what to say. Your father is Poseidon? You are a child of the sea? How could I be so stupid?" I dropped my head into my hands, hiding my face from him. How did I not see that? His love of the water, the sailing abilities...it all should have added up way before now.

"Wait, Zoey, what? You aren't stupid. What are you talking about?" He lifted my chin gently with a finger, so our eyes met. I could feel his need for eye contact.

"I can't believe I didn't see it before. It's amazing. And of course, I don't regret our kiss. I feel even more connected to you since you shared your...I'm not sure what to call it...abn ormality? Secret? I think it's fantastic!" I thought his gift was incredible. He just seemed to get more and more fascinating every day.

He grabbed me and pressed his lips to mine. "I'm so glad you're not upset with me. I don't think I could take it if you were."

He leaned forward to kiss me again. Something about his comment stuck with me. I pushed away.

"But you said 'visited.' Does that mean you no longer see your mother?" As soon as the words were out of my mouth, I regretted them. I could tell by his face that it was not something he would discuss and that just by uttering those words, I had hurt him.

"I'm so sorry. You don't have to talk about it. Just forget I asked."

"It's fine. Please, let me walk you back to your room," Kyro was polite, but the pain sat just under the surface.

I was pretty sure he would go back out to the water as soon as I was safely inside. I wasn't sure how I would find out about his mother, but I knew he wouldn't be the one to tell me.

I went to bed that night with stars in my eyes, thinking I would dream of Kyro and our time on the ship together. I couldn't have been more wrong. I had been sucked into another one of those strange realistic dreams. This time I came to in a dungeon, chained to the wall by my arms and legs. I was dressed in rags that barely pushed back the cold of the stone wall at my back. The dim light coming from torches on the wall barely lit the room enough to see the table set up in front of me. There looked to be tools on it, and with a look to my left and right, I realized I wasn't alone. After the last time, I was confident that this wasn't a dream...I was actually in this dungeon somehow. I tried to push that feeling away and convince myself this wasn't happening.

"Please, can you help me?" I softly called to one of the beings to my left. A groan was the only response. The being's head turned toward me, and for a moment, it looked as though Kyro was chained to the wall at my left. "Kyro? Is that you?" I shook my head in disbelief, and when I looked again, it was just a man I'd never seen before. He looked as though he had been beaten and tortured. I knew I was in trouble, but I had no idea how to escape.

I looked to my right and tried to solicit help from that side next. "Please. Is there anything you can do to help me?" This being turned to look at me, and for a moment, Q's face was staring back at me. Or at least most of it. It looked as though the right half of her face had been ripped off. All that remained of that side was a bloody mess marred with three claw marks.

This being had been tortured worse than the one on the left. I closed my eyes and shook my head. When I looked again, it was just a woman who was roughly the same size as Q, and I had never seen her before either. Sadly, the damage to her face stayed when she morphed from looking like Q to whoever she was. This whole thing had to be an illusion.

"It's cute how you think I'm not in control, my dear." I knew that voice. That was the voice from the nightmare I'd had after our encounter with the spiders. Oh, no! Was I captured for real this time? I could feel the cold steel of the cuffs on my wrists and ankles digging into my flesh. This had to be authentic. It couldn't be explained away as a dream—not this time.

"What do you want from me?" I asked as if I didn't already know that the book was the goal here.

"I've decided I want to add you to my collection, in addition to that book you've become so fond of lately." I shuddered as I realized I had no way out of this one. He must have learned after last time that I would fight and run to escape. I was also sure that my seeing Kyro and Q in the other prisoners' faces was intentional. I wasn't giving up; I just needed a plan. I wouldn't easily be added to his collection, but I wouldn't give him the satisfaction of arguing with him either.

"How can I give you the book if I'm stuck in this dream?" I figured it couldn't hurt to try to get some answers.

"This isn't a dream, and once you give your word that I'll have the book, a simple spell will send you back to retrieve it for me." I shuddered again. I wasn't sure I could lie my way out of this. "If you don't wish to cooperate, I can be persuasive."

With that, a hooded figure appeared with a whip in his hand. Suddenly I was chained to a rack instead of the wall. The hooded figure started cracking the whip, each time getting closer and closer to me. "What are you doing? You think torture will get you what you want?"

I knew antagonizing this crazy person wasn't in my best interest, but I couldn't just take being tortured without trying to fight back. And since my captor was a disembodied voice, I figured I'd try fighting with words.

"I'm certain torture will get me what I want, child. You will submit to me. Or you will die here. It's that simple." And with that, the hooded figure began to crack the whip across my back. Each lash dug into my flesh, ripping chunks out. I could feel the blood seeping from the wounds. I shouldn't have been able to feel pain in a dream. If I hadn't known before, I was convinced now that this was not a dream. After a few lashes, I passed out from the pain.

twenty-five

Kyro

When Zoey didn't come out of her room in the morning, Q and I got worried. We went to her room, and Q knocked softly. There was no response. "Should we go in and make sure she's OK?" I didn't want to invade her privacy, but I felt a panicked need to make sure she was alright.

"Yeah, we're going in." Q didn't seem too worried about privacy. I guessed Zoey wouldn't mind, given that it was late in the day and we were worried sick.

I opened the door, calling softly to her. "Zoey, are you awake?" There was no response, but I could hear her breathing. That was a good sign, at least. Q pushed past me and entered the room. I walked in after her and went to the window to open the curtains. Zoey was still sleeping and didn't budge when the light hit her. I was even more concerned at this point. Q walked over to her and grabbed her wrist to check her pulse. "Hey, Kyro, come look at this." She loosened her grip on Zoey's wrist like she was scared to hurt her.

I walked over from the window, and there was no question that something was wrong. Zoey's wrists were bleeding as though she had been tied or shackled and had fought against the restraints. "Oh, Zoey. Please wake up so you can tell us what happened." She stirred slightly but didn't wake. We tried smelling salts and a cold, damp cloth on her face, shaking her gently. None of it worked. Neither Q nor I knew what to do to wake her. She began to convulse, and we turned her on her side in case she started throwing up. It was then that we noticed the blood on her back. Q lifted her nightgown to reveal lash marks from a whip, and they looked fresh. It didn't make any sense how she could have new injuries from sleeping. I needed to get help. This was becoming a life or death situation. I knew we didn't have much time.

I knew I would have to go to my father and ask for Isa to come to check Zoey out. Isa was my father's healer and should know instantly what the problem was. Q decided to sit with Zoey while I was gone. She had already cleaned the wrist wounds and bound them with soft bandages. Shortly after she was finished, we discovered similar wounds on Zoey's ankles. Q took care of these as well while I prepared to go to the bottom of the ocean. I told Q that I would be back as soon as possible, and I got Mateo to stay on the boat with them for extra protection.

I stripped down and then dove into the water. I felt the familiar change as it occurred. There was the heat and the usual pain as my legs fused and my lungs adapted to the water. Once my tail had emerged, I was able to breathe underwater and could head to my father's court. It was a long journey, but I didn't slow down for fear of losing my one chance at love because I took a break. I was out of breath and exhausted when I got there, but I went straight to Father.

"I need your help. You told me before that this mission was too important to leave to chance. I hope you meant that." I bowed low in front of the King of the Seas.

"I do appreciate the show of respect, son, but you know that isn't necessary. Tell me what you need." My father was stern but kind and had the biggest heart of anyone I knew. I was confident he would help. And I knew that if I didn't show due respect, it could cause others to be disrespectful, and he wouldn't be happy about it. So no matter what he claimed, I would always bow low when I came to see him, especially when I was asking for his help to save the woman I loved.

"It's Zoey, the girl you sent me to help. She's asleep, or knocked out, or…I'm not sure, Father, but we can't wake her up, and she has injuries. There's no telling what's happening to her right now. Can Isa come with me to help her?" His face showed concern and then disappointment. I wasn't able to read what he was thinking. I desperately needed him to help me and wasn't sure what I would do if he didn't.

"My son, I can't send Isa up there. She doesn't have a human form. You know this. I'm sorry." His eyes shone with tears.

"But Father, can't you make an exception, just this one time? Can't you just give her legs for one day? It has to be possible. Please." I didn't want to beg, but I would if it meant saving Zoey.

"Kyro, you know I can't. That is the one thing that is outside my realm of power. A mermaid without a human ancestor cannot take a human form. It cannot be done. Do you forget the stories of your older half-sister who tried to bargain with the sea witch for that very thing? I know that happened way before your time, but the stories are well known. It did not end well for her, and it would not end well for Isa. I cannot ask that of her. I will not ask that of her, and neither will you. She cannot go onto land as a human."

I knew the stories he spoke of but had thought them legends to keep us away from the old sea witch until this point. Maybe there was a thread of truth to the tales after all. "What can I do, Father? Without Isa, I'm sure Zoey will die. I can't let that happen. I love her." Ah, there was the look I had hoped for, the look that told me I would get my way.

"Well, that does change things. But I still can't give Isa a human form. I will allow her to accompany you to the surface only if she agrees. You will have to bring your girl into the water and let Isa work on her there. That is the best I can do for you, son." He closed his eyes against the tears I could see forming and bowed his head at me.

"Thank you, Father. I will speak with Isa now. I'm sure she will help." I climbed the steps to the throne and hugged my father around his neck. He wrapped his arms around me as well, just for a moment.

I swam as fast as I could to Isa's chamber. I knew her well enough to know that she'd do anything to help. "Isa! Are you in there? I need you!" I called to her as I knocked.

She answered the door with her bag strapped across her chest. "Are you ready to go? I've been waiting all day for you to get here. Ari told me."

I almost collapsed in relief. "Thank you. So much." She had braided her russet hair to tame it. I kissed her cheek, and we headed up to the surface.

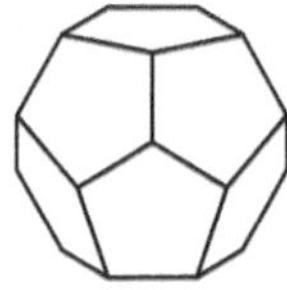

Once we had everyone in place, Isa checked Zoey out. "It's an astral projection spell. She didn't cast it, and I'm not sure I can break it. A mighty wizard did this. I've never seen power like this before. The good news is that she's fighting it—the wounds wouldn't show up on her body if she weren't fighting. Will you be able to hold her while I try to pull her back?"

Q and I looked at each other, and before we could say anything, Mateo responded. "We'll manage. You do what you have to; we can take turns holding her."

We traded off holding Zoey every three hours for the next two days. There were moments when we thought Isa would give up and moments when we thought Zoey would. Just when I was about to call it—Isa was exhausted—Zoey started to stir.

twenty-six

Isa

WHEN KYRO SHOWED UP, I had been expecting him. Ari and I kept close tabs on our boy and knew he was in trouble. I also knew that Poseidon wouldn't make me go to help. What

I didn't expect was that he wouldn't stop me from going. He wasn't much on letting any of us help humans or other species. We were made to keep pretty much to ourselves and take care of the oceans' creatures. Most of us were OK with that, but there were a few who wanted to help everyone.

I had my bag packed and ready. I was prepared to cause a distraction and sneak out. Ari and I had it all planned out. So when Poseidon just allowed me to go, it was unnerving. I was sure this meant that the girl was more important than we had initially thought. It wasn't often that Kyro asked for help, and even less often that Poseidon gave it.

It took almost a day to get back to the ship. I knew this would be difficult since I wasn't able to transform into a human. When we arrived, they brought Zoey into the water, and I did an examination. The cause of her current state was a potent astral projection spell, and I wasn't convinced I could get through the wards, much less break the spell and bring her back. I knew I had to try, for Kyro's sake. I set up my crystal grid, cast a circle, and got to work.

I held onto Zoey, closed my eyes, and sent myself forth in astral form. This part was a little bit like walking down a narrow hallway, or in my case, swimming. Fortunately for me, my cosmic self didn't need water for that. I just floated as though the air around me was water. I followed the path into the astral trap where Zoey was contained. I was unable to enter it at first because it was heavily warded. I had to fight my way through. I conjured up a sword and began hacking at the spider-web-like threads that connected each point of the wards, attempting to break the containment spell.

Inside the astral plane, time flows differently than it does on Earth. What seemed like hours to me in here would be mere minutes out there to everyone else. Or it could be precisely the opposite, where it seemed like moments to me, but days or weeks to outsiders. There was no natural way to tell how this would go. I thought that I would need to remember to do a memory wipe on Zoey once I got her out. There was no telling what kind of horrors she had witnessed or been through inside. I wouldn't let her suffer if I could prevent it. I continued slicing through the ward threads of the spell until every one of them had been severed. Then I floated through the door.

Instantly, I was inside a cold, damp dungeon. It was dark, with only a couple of small candles for light. I cast a protective bubble to shield myself from being seen or harmed and then began to make my way around the room, looking for Zoey. There were several prisoners chained in different places along the walls. The lack of light made it more difficult to tell which one was her. Most of them were conjurations, but there were a few who were astrally trapped like Zoey. Each one I came across, I set free from their chains. For some, I could unfasten their manacles, but I had to use my sword to break the chains for others.

I was beginning to lose hope of finding Zoey. After freeing half a dozen other trapped souls, I was searching the final corner of the room. It was the darkest area, but I sensed three forms. I floated closer and came face to face with a siren that had been transformed to look like Q. Half of her face had been mutilated, and she was near death. There was no way she would be able to get herself out of here even if I freed her. Yet, one look into her eyes, and I couldn't leave her. I unlatched her manacles and set her free. Her eyes caught mine, and I knew she was thanking me. I hugged her tightly, told her all would be well and ran my sword through her gut. The siren dissolved instantly. I took comfort in the fact that she would no longer suffer, and at some point, would be reincarnated into another sea creature.

I didn't have time to worry about my actions; I had to find Zoey. I walked past a body slumped chained to the wall and checked the next prisoner. It was a male, and upon inspection, he was a conjuration that looked surprisingly like Kyro. That meant Zoey was here. She had to be close. I turned back to the slumped body. It was the only one I hadn't checked. It had to be her. I rushed over.

Sure enough, it was her. At that moment, I was relieved because I found her, but terrified because I didn't know if she was still alive. She was hanging by her wrists, with her ankles bound as well. Her head was slumped over onto her chest, and I couldn't tell if she was breathing or not. "Zoey, are you alright?" I tried to keep my voice calm and soft. I didn't want to frighten her.

"I already told you...leave me alone. I'm not joining you no matter what you do to me. Go away." She spoke so softly, but it was hard to miss the venom in her words. My heart broke with their meaning. She had been tortured.

I moved closer and used only my index finger; I lifted her chin to see her face. "Oh, dear one, we've all been so worried. I've come to take you back." Her poor face was scraped, and there was dried blood on her lip. One of her eyes may have been black, but it was too dark to tell for sure. Once she looked at me, her expression changed a bit. "Is it you, Isa? Or is this some trick?" Her voice softened with vulnerability for a moment.

I went to work unlocking the manacles at her feet first, then the ones around her hands. She was too weak to stand, so I knew I would have to carry her. "It's OK, child, I'm here. I'll carry you out—just lean on me." She nodded defeatedly and let me slide myself under her arm. Even in the astral plane, she was heavy. She was almost a foot taller than me, so it was awkward at best. I had to take it slow and be quiet to avoid letting her captor know she was missing. As I picked her up, I expanded my protective bubble into surrounding her as well. Carefully I moved toward the door.

I didn't expect to make it out without a fight. Unfortunately, I was right. I made it to the door carrying Zoey before the attack came. Somehow, whoever had taken her managed to get through my protection bubble. That wasn't good because it meant we were dealing with a mighty being. I realized this as Zoey, and I got slammed into the door from behind. I eased her down to lean against the door, then turned to face the attacker. Of course, it was the other prisoners from the dungeon we were in.

There were three of them total attacking me. Luckily they were the conjurations, so I didn't have to worry about having another murder on my conscience. As soon as the thought crossed my mind, I knew I had to shield my thoughts better because all three of them morphed into the girl I had killed a few minutes ago. Now there were three of her. Each one was hitting, clawing, and kicking at me. I knew they would do whatever they could to stop me from taking Zoey out of here. I tried to fight back with the sword I had conjured up, but it just sliced right through them. I started to panic. I tried my fists and feet next, with the same results. There was nothing I could do to hit these things. I had no idea how to defeat these creatures if my weapon wouldn't work.

I knew I needed to calm down and make sure I protected Zoey. I couldn't do that if I were freaking out. I stopped for a minute to think. What would Kyro tell me to do? What would Poseidon say? I knew both would give the same answer. Calm your mind, focus on the light inside, and create a stronger shield. I may not defeat these monsters, but I could surely conjure up stronger protection and cover myself and Zoey with it. And maybe if I focused hard enough, I could create a ball of light to blind them while I made the shield. I laid Zoey down behind me and started to meditate.

"I know this isn't the best time for this, Zoey, but I promise it's to protect you," I whispered to the barely conscious girl on the floor. Then I closed my eyes and pictured a small ball of light in my open palms. I focused on it getting bigger and bigger until it was as large as I was tall. I could feel the light touching my skin, and the sounds of the creatures got quieter. I knew this was my chance to make the shield. I changed my focus to creating a more structured protection bubble around myself and Zoey, making sure it was solid and impenetrable this time. Once I had it in place, I opened my eyes to take a look. Not bad if I do say so myself. I picked Zoey up again and opened the door.

We still had to make it down the hallway and out of wherever this was. I hoped the ball of light would buy us some time. I half dragged Zoey down the hallway toward the light that would lead us back to our bodies. I heard a commotion behind us, and upon turning my head to see what it was, I realized that I should have at least closed the door. Following us toward the light were three demons, no longer taking on the appearance of the girl I'd killed. Now they looked terrifying, covered in blood and open wounds. They screeched as they chased us farther and farther down the hallway. I had to make it to the end before they caught us. I wasn't sure I was strong enough to do it. I realized that it might be necessary for me to stay so Zoey could get out. I started the chant for the memory wipe spell as I ran. At least I could make her forget the horrors of this place when she awoke, whether or not I was there.

Just as I completed the spell, the monsters were right behind us, and I was losing steam. I had to push energy into Zoey so she could escape. Once I gave her the boost, she came to and realized she had to run. I turned to face the monsters, giving her a chance to escape. "Run, Zoey!" I yelled at her. The shield I had conjured up was slowing the creatures down, but they kept coming. I knew I wouldn't be able to hold them off much longer. I would have to take my chances and run. I dropped the shield to run; the creatures were hit with a beam of ice that came from behind me.

"Come on, Isa, we have to go!" Zoey had come back to get me. I couldn't believe she would risk herself that way. We held hands and ran down the hallway to the end, and then we had to split off to get back to our bodies.

"You go first, and I'll close the connection so they can't get to you." I shoved her toward her door.

"OK, but you'll be right behind? And you'll close the connection on your side, too, right?" It was touching that she cared so much for me, given that we hadn't spent much time together.

"Yes, I will. Now go!" She ran through her door. It closed behind her, and I performed the short ritual for closing the connection. Then I ran to my door and did the same thing. Now it was just a matter of waiting to see when she woke up.

I came back into my body as if I had never left. Kyro was holding Zoey, and Q was watching from the boat deck. Mateo was close by me to make sure I didn't get swept away by a wave in the middle of the healing process.

twenty-seven

Zoey

I woke up in the ocean, in Kyro's arms. The first thing I saw was the russet-haired mermaid with the sunset tail. What was her name again? I'd only seen her a couple of times and met her once. Isabella, I think it was. "What's going on? Why am I in the water? What happened?" Kyro looked as though he had seen a ghost. He pulled me close and kissed me hard. "I'm so glad you're back!" I looked around, confused, and saw Q leaning over the boat's railing, watching me. I wasn't sure why my head was so foggy. And waking up in the water was highly disturbing. It must have been evident from the look on my face.

"We thought you were dying. Kyro had to get help. Isa has been here for two days working on healing you. You've been out for almost four days total." Q was blunt as ever, but it was a relief. I couldn't remember exactly what had happened, but there was a dark shadow in my memory, and it terrified me.

"You won't remember anything right now, if at all." It was as though Isa could read my mind.

"How did you know?"

She laughed, "The look on your face said it all. It's OK. You're safe now."

Then Isa turned to Kyro and kissed him on the cheek. "Mateo, will you escort me home? I'm feeling a bit weak and could use the company." Then she turned back to Kyro. "Let me know if you need anything else. You know I'm happy to help." And with that, Isa and Mateo headed back under the water, leaving me to figure out what was going on.

We pulled into the dock and anchored the boat. We were in a small port in South Africa, where Kyro had some friends. Our journey had been long and quiet so far, except for the mermaid visits each evening. I met each of them and watched Kyro swim and play with them in the water. It was a nice break in the monotony of sailing on the ocean. Kyro was concerned about running out of supplies before we made it to Japan, and I think Q was getting tired of boat life as well.

We left the boat to meet up with Kyro's friends and gather supplies. There was an open-air market set up a few yards from the docks. We strolled over to see if we could find the food and supplies that we would need. Kyro kept an eye out for his friends while we shopped. I could tell he was feeling nervous about this stop, even though it was necessary.

He asked a few of the vendors if they had seen Gill and Mack. It was a small village, and the vendors he asked knew them. They pointed us toward the village center, past the market, toward the jungle that surrounded it. We decided to venture that way and see if Kyro could find the information he was looking for.

Q decided to check out the pub and see if anyone had any information on our destination. Kyro and I walked on, heading toward Gill's hut on the edge of the village.

When we got there, Kyro motioned for me to stop and be silent. I looked around to see what had set him on edge. The door of the hut was half-open, and the one-room cabin was a disaster inside. It was hard to tell if it had been ransacked or if Gill was that much of a slob. I was guessing from Kyro's reaction, it was the former and not the latter.

Once he was satisfied that we weren't in immediate danger, he motioned for me to follow him inside to look around. We found the entire place had been tossed as though someone was searching for something of value. It appeared the item in question had not been located, as there were streaks of blood on the floor. The scene looked like Gill may have been beaten or tortured to extract information.

Kyro thought we should follow the trail and see if we could help his friend. I agreed but asked if we could find Q first so we would have some backup. With my lack of experience fighting, he agreed.

Once we had found Q brought her up to speed about what we suspected, we were on our way—following the sparse blood drops into the dense foliage of the jungle. We came to a slight clearing, where it looked as though a lean-to structure had been constructed against a pair of trees, with a campfire nearby. We could see what appeared to be a figure lying on the ground under the lean-to. Kyro wanted to burst through the leaves into the open and surprise whoever was there. Q suggested that we hold back for a bit and observe the area. I opted to go with Q's idea because she seemed to have the most experience with this kind of situation because of the three of us.

"I don't see why we can't just go get him. He's tied up and laying under that lean-to. Let's go." Kyro was persistent.

"How can you be sure that's Gill?" I wasn't even sure that it was a person, much less Kyro's friend. "I just know. It has to be him." Kyro was getting impatient.

Q was just as persistent, if not more so. "There has to be someone or something guarding him. He's not alone. We can't just burst out there and grab him. We don't even know if he can run or not. We don't know anything about the situation at the moment except that your friend may be tied up. Who knows? That could be a trap. How well do you know this guy?"

Kyro looked seriously offended by the question. "I grew up with him. I've known him almost my entire life. He and Mack are my best friends. How can you even suspect that he would do something to harm us? Especially when he had no idea we were coming."

"Kyro is right," I interjected before this could escalate into a bigger problem than it already was. "And Q is right. We have to help Gill, but we have to be careful. We can't just snatch and grab, but we can try to get a better vantage point and see if we can get him out of here. It would be easier if we knew what we're up against."

"OK," Kyro sounded somewhat defeated, but I think he understood my point. "I'm just worried about him, and I want to make sure he's alright."

"That will be easier if we keep an eye out and see who or what has him. We don't want a repeat of the cavern, do we?" I didn't even want to think of running into more of those giant spiders.

Kyro simply nodded. We carefully worked our way around the clearing, moving closer to the lean-to, so we could see Gill and decide how to help him best. Once we got to the best vantage point, we could see that it looked as though his hands and feet were tied. He seemed to be sleeping, which was a good thing. It meant he was alive.

We opted to wait and watch for a while to see what we were up against. It was apparent Gill was being held prisoner, but there were no guards in sight. That probably meant we were dealing with a magical cell and wouldn't be able to get him out very quickly.

After waiting for what seemed like hours, we heard rustling on the opposite side of the clearing. At this point, we had climbed a couple of trees—Kyro and I in one, Q in another—for a safer observation point. We could see the clearing and would be out of sight of whoever or whatever came out.

It was a good thing Kyro was with me when I saw what emerged from the leaves. His hand was over my mouth before I had a chance to gasp—or worse, scream.

It was around six feet tall, humanoid, with gray-looking fish scales covering its exposed skin. It was wearing pants with no shirt. Its face looked like a weird combination of fish and man, with a flattened nose and gray fins on either side of its head where its ears should be. I could see the muscles in its arms flex as it headed toward Gill, who was still sleeping or knocked out.

"Get up!" It hissed at Gill, who didn't respond. The fish-man walked over and kicked Gill's boot. He groaned and moved his hands to his head as though the vibration of the kick caused him pain. "I said, get up, NOW!" The fish-man was getting impatient with Gill.

Before I could stop him, Kyro had jumped from the tree onto the fish man's back. He tried to knock it out with a chokehold, but the fish man tried to flip Kyro over and off its back. Q jumped out of her tree, motioned for me to stay put, and crept over to stand behind the fish man with Kyro on his back. She rubbed her hands together, said something under her breath, and suddenly her hands glowed with flames that shot out onto the fish-man's legs. Realizing what was happening, Kyro changed his tactic from trying to subdue the fish man to simply snapping its neck.

While they dealt with the body, I carefully climbed out of the tree and crept over to where Gill was lying. He was still holding his head as though he was scared and waiting for the next blow. I leaned down and laid a hand gently on his shoulder. "Shhh, it's alright, we're here now."

His whimpers stopped, his hands came down, and he looked up at me in awe. "Goddess Amyria, you heard my prayers. Thank you."

"You are welcome, but I am not a goddess. I am simply a friend of Kyro, and I hope to be a friend of yours. Come, let's get out of here." He seemed calmed by my presence, which was nice. It made getting him out of there a lot easier than if he had stayed in shock.

I cut his hands and feet free and helped him to stand up. Now that I had a better vantage point, I could get a good look at his injuries. He had a black eye and a few scrapes on his left cheek, but nothing was majorly wrong.

I then guided him to where Kyro was consulting with Q. They were trying to decide if they should look for fish man's friends. I put that thought to rest when Gill and I walked over. "We have to take him back to his village. He isn't safe here." With that, I turned and guided Gill back toward his home. Kyro and Q followed.

We started on the most direct route, which took us to the edge of a small village. It was the afternoon, and no one was out. There was no indication of danger, so we walked into the town, watching everything at once. Gill was still in shock and wasn't talking.

"Are we going the right way?" I turned to Kyro and Gill since they seemed to know this place better than Q or myself. Gill didn't respond; he had this absent look on his face as though he wasn't even with us.

"I think so, but I'm not sure." Well, getting lost in the jungle wasn't on my list of things to do today, but here we were.

"Perhaps we should backtrack and go around this village." Q chimed in. "I have a bad feeling."

At that moment, a figure came out of one of the huts in front of us. It was another fish-man. It seemed Q's feeling had been right. Before we could run, he started yelling and charged at us. I couldn't understand the language he was speaking, but I was pretty confident he was letting others know that there were intruders in the village. Kyro, Q, and I made a circle around Gill, with our backs facing him to protect him from the attackers that had started coming out of other huts. We were surrounded. I counted at least a dozen fish-men, with more coming up the path.

We fought hard, but even when Gill snapped out of it and fought with us, it wasn't enough. Q wore herself out using her fire magic, and I wasn't an experienced enough fighter to be much help. If we got out of this, I was going to make them train me. Two of the fish-men caught Q first, since she was weakened, and tied her arms behind her back before smacking her in the head with a small club to knock her out. They got Gill next, much in the same way. It was just Kyro, and I left. I kept swinging and kicking, but one of the fish-men caught my leg mid-kick, and the next thing I knew, I was flat on my back. I guess I was seen as less of a threat because they didn't bother to knock me out. Once I was captured, Kyro surrendered willingly, and they decided not to knock him out either. I guess they realized I could be used as a bargaining chip to keep him in line.

The fish-men took us deeper into the jungle. Kyro and I were forced to walk while they wheeled Gill and Q in carts that would have been used for firewood. I lost track of how many turns we took as we headed into the heart of the jungle. The heat had started to get to me, and I had stopped sweating. I knew I was becoming dehydrated, but the fish-men weren't too concerned about our comfort. I felt terrible for Kyro since he was used to being in or near the water. I thought being this far inland might even affect his powers.

We came upon a cave deep in the jungle, and the fish-men shoved us inside. It was dark and damp, which was nice compared to the heat and humidity outside. There were cages along the walls of the cave, most of which were empty. There were a few with bodies inside; it was impossible to tell if the beings were alive, though. Kyro was forced into one of the cages, and I was locked in the one next to him. Q was put into the next one, and Gill the one after that. Once we were shoved inside, they untied my hands, along with Kyro's and Gill's. I figured they weren't taking any chances with Q since she had fried as many of them as she could while we fought.

There was nothing for us to do or discuss with our captors standing next to the cages, so we decided to rest. Sleep came, but it was fitful and didn't last long. I felt the pull of the darkness that had taken me before. I fought it as hard as I could since I didn't want to be kidnapped again. This time I was able to resist, though I'm not quite sure how I did it. I woke to a hazy bubble surrounding me. I looked around for the source, and the guards were gone. Gill was awake, staring at me and murmuring something inaudible.

"Gill? Are you alright?" I called to him softly, in case our guards were still close enough to hear. He closed his eyes and shook his head a little. When his eyes opened again, they were clear, and it was apparent he was better. "I woke while you were sleeping. It looked as though you were being pulled apart, so I cast a bubble. It prevented your soul from leaving your body. I'm not sure what it was, but I managed to stop it for now."

Well, at least now I knew how the ominous voice and the creature it belonged to managed to trap me. I would need to look into something to keep my soul attached to my body during sleep. "Thank you." Gill nodded, then sat back down on the floor. His back was to me, and it looked like he was going to sleep.

I sat down as well, but I wasn't going to sleep. I was trying to come up with a plan for our escape.

TWENTY-EIGHT

Gill

After putting Zoey's mind at ease, I sat down against the bars of the cage, with my back to her. I needed to report in and couldn't astral project if the others could tell what I was doing. Before her nightmare began, I had started the process and cut myself off when I realized what was happening. I had to cooperate, but that didn't mean she had to suffer. I closed my eyes and relaxed my body. My mind began to wander, but I pulled it back and focused on the dark room I needed to project myself into. I knew he would be there waiting. I was reasonably sure he would be pissed that I interrupted his spell. I would deal with the fallout from that. It was the least I could do, given the circumstances.

I projected my consciousness into the specified room. I was met with an angry image. He hadn't met me in person since I was recruited, and for that, I was grateful. His magic was less powerful here, and I was sure he could not kill me in the dream world. "Why did you stop me? You know you'll be punished for that." The voice was even angrier than the face.

"Why did you have these goons kidnap me? And my friends? You could have just let us go. I told you I'd get the book."

The angry face seemed to calm a bit, though I was still sure this was not the face of the man who was blackmailing me. "Would you have me make it easy for you? Where's the fun in that?" He scoffed. Then he let loose a dark laugh that hinted at mania.

"I know this isn't going to be easy, but how can I get the book if we are trapped in cages, and she doesn't have it with her? You can't just have the fish minions let us go. That would make the others suspicious." I was getting irritated at how difficult he wanted this to be for me, though he held my life over my head. He knew I had no choice but to do his bidding.

"I've already made the guards leave. They will make daily rounds to keep up appearances, of course. All you have to do is convince your friends to break out of the cages between these rounds. That shouldn't be too difficult for you." He chuckled again, and I knew it wouldn't be that easy. Once free of the cages, we'd have to fight our way out of the jungle. "You know what I want, now get it for me, or else." The next thing I knew, my consciousness was thrust back into my body, and I was slammed against the bars of my cell.

I had to play it off as though I had a bad dream and had awoken with a startle. Luckily for me, it had appeared to the others that I had been the fish men's captive for a while and had suffered some torture. It wasn't outside the realm of possibility for me to have some traumatic memories to deal with. I just had to play it up by refusing to talk about what had happened to me and acting scared of our captors. I had been lying for so long that I wasn't even sure what the truth was anymore.

I sat there pondering what my punishment would be since there was no explanation. I knew it could happen at any time, and there would be no warning. I was sure that no matter what it was, defying him again would make it worse. As would outright rebellion, which was entirely out of the question.

I turned to face the others, who were starting to wake. Except for Zoey—she looked as though she hadn't slept at all. I guessed that this wasn't the first time she'd been astrally abducted, and the damage from it showed on her face. Now it was just a matter of convincing the three of them to break out of these cages.

Kyro was the first to speak. "How long have you been awake?" he asked Zoey first, probably because she looked the worst off.

"A while. The guards haven't come around since I woke." Her voice was laced with sadness that penetrated my soul.

"I woke before her, and the guards weren't around then either." Q looked uncomfortable with her hands bound behind her. "My head is killing me. Where are we?"

We took turns explaining to her where we were and what had happened since she'd been knocked out. Then we set out to formulate a plan of escape. It was hard not to tell the others that I knew the guards weren't coming back until dark. There was no way to explain that knowledge without giving away my true purpose, so I had to let it go.

The others needed proof of the pattern that I had been told of, so we watched for the guards to come back. As we did so, Q worked on freeing her hands to pick the cage locks. The fish-men weren't concerned with us escaping, so they hadn't taken any of our supplies. No one seemed to think that was weird. I didn't mention it to keep from drawing attention to an apparent oversight.

Q worked on her cage first, taking the better part of an hour to figure out how to pick the lock. We had decided she would free me next, and I would keep watch while she worked on the others. Since my cage was the farthest back in the cave, it wouldn't be evident to our captors that I wasn't in it until after they were inside. Of course, I knew that wasn't going to be an issue. Once I was free, I snuck to the mouth of the cave anyway and pretended to keep watch. I had to make sure I appeared to be nervous, which was pretty easy given that I could be punished at any time in any way.

It took her half the day, but Q finally got Kyro's and Zoey's cages opened. After much discussion, we decided it would be better to leave after knowing the guards' pattern. So even though we were free, we were trapped. We spent some time exploring the cave before we put ourselves back in the cages. Q had made sure to break the locks so that we couldn't get trapped inside again. We just had to look like prisoners for a while before we made our move.

The guards came in the evening, threw fruit at our cages, and then left again. It was exactly as I was told. Escape should be easy. We quietly opened the cage doors and crept to the mouth of the cave. I looked outside to the left and right, and there was nothing to be seen. It was dusk and just starting to get dark out.

I knew I had to convince them to leave soon. We needed to get back to the boat, so I could steal the book before it was too late. I was getting frustrated that they all wanted to wait longer to execute our escape. "It's fine, Kyro. Just forget that I've had your back for longer than you've known these women," I spat. "And just forget that I've saved your life multiple times over the decades we've known each other." I was on the verge of losing my temper and blowing the whole plan. I went back to my cell to calm down.

"What's his problem?" Q didn't get what I was saying.

"He's fine. He can be a bit overzealous when he thinks he's right. I'll go talk to him." At least Kyro would give me a private moment. Perhaps I could convince him after all. I waited as he slowly closed the distance between us. I didn't even look up when he came in and sat down beside me.

"Gill, man, what's up? This isn't like you." His voice was low, as though he didn't want the girls to hear us.

"I'm just trying to help, Kyro." I looked up at him expectantly.

"We've been going over the plan for hours. The guards haven't come back. I just really think we should leave now while there's still a small amount of daylight left and before the guards come back." I tried to keep the desperation out of my voice.

"I know you think that's best, but we're just not sure. And insulting the girls isn't going to convince them to listen to you.

We all have to agree to the plan because it affects us all." Ever the diplomat, Kyro made sense.

I would have to try a different tactic to get him on my side. Maybe desperation was just what I needed. "I'm sorry, Kyro, I just don't want to be stuck here anymore. I'm scared that they'll come back and torture me more like they did before you came." I made sure my voice cracked at the end to make my emotion believable. I desperately needed him to trust me.

"I'll talk to the girls and see if they'll agree to leave now. If your intuition says we need to go now, I trust you. Just be patient with them, OK? We will get out of here, I promise." With that, he stood up and walked out of the cell. I tried to listen in as he talked to Zoey and Q, but they kept their voices low, and I couldn't make out what was being said.

It didn't take long to find out. Even though I had pissed her off, after talking to Kyro, Q had sided with me against him, and she had convinced Zoey to agree as well. I guess trusting me wasn't enough to abandon his intuition. I knew this wouldn't be as easy as the angry one had made it sound.

I could tell Kyro was uneasy, but he agreed to go along with what everyone wanted. We crept out of the cave one by one, half expecting an ambush. When one didn't happen, we relaxed a bit, and I began to lead everyone back to my village.

twenty-nine

In total, we'd been held captive by the fish-men for three days. Our escape was made at Gill's insistence at the end of the third day, though we'd been free of the cages for almost two days. Those locks were more complex than I'm used to, and it frustrated me that beating them took me so long.

I began to suspect Gill may not have been on our side when he led us into the fish heads' village. I wasn't about to accuse him without proof, so I kept my eyes open and mouth shut. Kyro came to me and explained how Gill was scared to stay because of the torture he'd been subjected to, so, of course, I changed my mind about waiting until morning to leave. It would be easier to prove that he was working with or for the fish faces if we were outside the cave. Kyro seemed suspicious of my sudden change of heart, especially when I convinced Zoey to go along with it for Gill's sake. Kyro even tried to argue that we should stay the night in the cave and leave in the morning. He probably could have just made the decision for us, but he had already made the mistake of saying it was a "majority rules" situation, and here we were...hiking.

We hiked in what Gill said was his village's direction until it was too dark to go on. Then I insisted that we make camp for the rest of the night. No one objected since none of us could see where we were going anyway. There was no way to tell if we were even going the right way.

We set up camp the best we could, considering we had very few supplies. Zoey helped Kyro create a makeshift shelter by weaving vines together. The idea was to keep from being in plain sight if the fish faces came hunting for us. Gill continued to insist that they wouldn't, but how could he be so sure?

Once we were set up, we decided to take turns keeping watch, so we didn't get ambushed. I took the first watch, and as I had already decided that I had to keep Gill from having a solo watch, I insisted that we do our watches in pairs. I convinced the others that it was a good idea because two sets of eyes were better than one, and we would keep each other awake better that way.

Kyro and Zoey got comfortable behind the lean-to and slept, while Gill attempted to avoid me without making it obvious. I wondered if he was afraid that I had already figured him out. I was confident I could get it out of him with enough time. I walked over to where he was sitting against the trunk of a tree.

"So exactly what makes you so sure the fish guys won't come after us?" I thought I'd lead with that and then see what I could get out of him.

"It's just a feeling. I have no way to know for sure. Shouldn't we be quiet so we can keep watch?" He didn't want to talk. It seemed as though he was pretty nervous too. Good. Anxious people make mistakes. All I had to do is trip him up.

"Come on; you were with those fish heads for days before we found you. And you didn't learn anything about why they kidnapped you or what they planned to do with you?" I thought that might be enough to convince him to open up.

"How would I know what they wanted? I was their prisoner. They didn't tell me why they were torturing me. I just thought they enjoyed hurting me." He got up and stormed off, mumbling under his breath. I could tell that I was starting to get to him; breaking him wouldn't be too hard.

I stayed where I was after he stalked away. I had a good vantage point of our little camp and him for the rest of my watch. I could see everything he was doing from this spot, which suited me just fine. It was hard to tell if he was giving up on watch and going to sleep with his back against a tree or if he was meditating. Either way, I was planning to keep an eye on him.

We sat in silence for a while before I heard them. A branch broke, and I was immediately on alert. Gill sat up suddenly, too, listening. I didn't bother the others just yet. I wanted to see what we were dealing with, so I hid in the bushes. My hiding spot was directly across from where Kyro and Zoey were sleeping. I noticed that Gill must have had the same idea, as he ducked behind some bushes on the other side of the makeshift lean-to.

It only took a moment for those approaching to get close enough to be visible. Of course, it was a couple of those fish guys tracking us. So either Gill was just wrong, or he was setting us up. I waited until they passed by and then crept over to wake Zoey and Kyro. I opted to wake them one at a time, which was a good plan, given Zoey's reaction. I had to clamp my hand over her mouth to keep her from screaming. Kyro woke pretty quietly but was instantly on alert. I couldn't see Gill anymore and wasn't sure if that would end up hurting us or not.

I whispered to Kyro what had happened and in which direction our scaly friends had gone. Then I explained that Gill had vanished in the chaos while the fish heads were walking through. I didn't tell Kyro about my suspicions regarding Gill because I didn't have any proof yet. We decided to look for Gill because two fish guys wouldn't be that hard to get rid of, and there was safety in numbers. We crept around the campsite, barely making a sound.

I heard a branch break right behind me, so I turned around and tackled the noisemaker. Gill had decided to come out from hiding and sneak upon us. I pinned him to the ground, trying to silence him before he attracted company. I knew it was pointless when I looked up and saw Zoey's and Kyro's faces. The fish heads were headed our way, and we only had a moment to prepare.

Each of us ducked behind a tree in a square pattern where we should have been able to flank the fish guys and capture them. Just as they rushed past me, I started to conjure up a fireball to take one of them out. Before I could release it, I got hit from behind. I lost concentration on the spell and hit the ground. The fish faces turned to see what the commotion was, and Kyro leaped on the back of one while Zoey swung a tree branch at the other one. Kyro's fish-man began to turn wildly in circles, trying to throw him. Zoey's went down with a blow to the face.

I struggled to my feet and looked around to see who had hit me. There was no one anywhere around me. I was pretty sure I knew who had done it, but again, I had no proof. It wasn't like I saw him standing over me while I was knocked on the ground. Why would he have saved a fish person, though? Didn't he just tell Kyro how badly their torture had affected him? Where was he anyway?

Kyro and Zoey managed to subdue the second fish guy and tied both of them up with vines. I walked around the area looking for Gill. I stopped when I heard voices. I was close enough to make out what was being said barely.

"This wasn't part of the deal." I was pretty sure that voice was Gill.

"Neither was you letting them kill all my followers." The second voice was dark and angry.

"I wasn't letting them...I kept her from making the fireball, didn't I? That should be good enough." I could tell Gill was irritated but scared.

"Just make sure you don't fail me and don't let them kill any more of my people. Now go!" I ducked behind a tree to avoid being seen as Gill ran past me to the clearing. After he passed, I poked my head around to see who he had been talking to, but no one was there.

I met the others back in the clearing, where we decided to leave the fish faces tied up and blindfolded. They couldn't follow us if they couldn't see where we went. Once we had the fish-men situated, we started hiking again. It was difficult in the dark, but there was no way we would try to camp. I debated if I should tell Kyro what I had heard but thought better of it. Without proof, I would just be the woman making wild accusations at his friend.

So we continued walking until we found the trail. The sun came up, and our travel got easier. It was apparent we were getting closer to the village. Kyro filled Gill in on why we happened to show up at just the right time and asked if he would be interested in continuing on our journey with us. I thought it was funny that he didn't mention the book—just saying that we were on a quest for a magical item that a wizard needed to save the world.

Zoey

NONE OF US SPOKE until we were back in the village center, past Gill's house, heading back to the docks. "Wait, we have to get Mack. He's at the stables. I'll go with you, but he needs to have the option to go as well." The second time he spoke to me, we rescued him, and Gill seemed back to normal.

"Of course, brother, we must go see Mack. I will need him as well." It was apparent Kyro loved his friends. We turned right down a path away from the jungle and headed toward the stables. I was excited to see horses face to face for the first time. There were so many new experiences on this planet. It made me sad that it was dying. But that's what we were trying to fix.

Mack was not at all what I expected. He was four-and-a-half feet tall, with broad shoulders, long red hair braided into two plaits down his back, and a full beard. I had read of dwarves but had yet to meet one until now. I honestly was under the impression they were myths. The moment he saw Kyro, he put down his hammer and horseshoe, walked over, and proceeded to give Kyro the tightest bear hug I had ever seen. Kyro didn't seem to mind and returned the hug with equal vigor.

Once he let go of Kyro, Mack grabbed me and hugged me like we'd known each other for our whole lives. I think Kyro could tell I wasn't used to this kind of affection, and he carefully dragged Mack off of me, apologizing for his friend. Mack gave Q a measured glance as if considering a hug for her as well and then shrugged as though he thought better of it. He then turned to us and addressed Kyro, "Ah, brother, you've found two mates and brought them for my approval. This one," as he gestured to me, "I like this one. But that one," now he motioned toward Q, "I don't think will be a good fit."

Kyro and Gill started laughing uncontrollably, while Q looked disinterested, and I'm sure that I looked mortified. Mack didn't seem to get what the laughter was for. "What? What are ye laughing about?"

Kyro responded, "Mack, my friend. You always did know how to greet a lady. But you're mistaken. Only one of them is mine. I've brought the other for you." He winked at Q as he said it, and she seemed willing to play along. Kyro continued, "Can you guess which is which?"

I realized this moment of levity was what we needed after what we'd just been through. I tried not to give away the answer, but I was sure my cheeks were glowing red with embarrassment. Just then, Q decided to come to my rescue. "C'mon, wee one, can't you tell that your friend brought me for you?" She winked at me as she said it and stepped toward Mack. He took a few steps backward and held up his hands.

"I'll pass on this one. She's not my type. Too much fire demon in her." Mack seemed for a brief second to be genuinely scared of Q. Once that passed, his eyes shone with mischief again, and he took my hand. "Wouldn't you at least consider running away with me and forgetting about him?"

I laughed at this obvious joke, and everyone seemed to relax a little. Soon enough, Mack and Gill were filled in on the mission and had chosen to come along. As we were chatting, I got a better look at Kyro's friends. Even after being on Calliope, it was strange for me to see so many different races getting along as though they were family. On the space station, most races kept to themselves by choice, with a few exceptions.

The three of them seemed so different yet got along like brothers. Gill was about five-foot-seven, with chestnut curls that barely touched his ears. He was stocky but not overweight and had a quiet demeanor. Mack was stocky as well, but his personality was almost directly in opposition with Gill's. He was loud and boisterous and somewhat offensive, without a care in the world for what anyone thought about him or his opinions. They were a fantastic mix. I hoped we would all get along on our journey.

We managed to get back to the boat with no issues. With two extra sets of hands, it took half the time to load up. We were on our way before darkness fell. It appeared that Gill, Mack, and Kyro had sailed together before. Each knew how to anticipate what the others were doing to keep the boat going in the right direction. Gill and Mack also shared a room with bunk beds, just down the hall from my room and across from Q's room, next to Kyro's.

Once sleeping arrangements had been settled, we decided it would be good to eat. Q and I offered to cook this time, with the understanding that it would not be a permanent arrangement. Of course, being hungry, the men all agreed. I was sure there'd be mutiny about it later because I knew the guys would rather have the ladies cook, but we'd deal with it when it came up. For now, we seemed like one big, happy family.

After filling our bellies, we agreed to get some sleep before talking about strategy on the mission's next step. I went back to the deck for some alone time after everyone had gone to their rooms. I sat on the deck with my feet hanging over the edge, just watching the water. It was nice to have an ordinary evening after all the chaos from the past few days. It was hard to reconcile that this was my life now. I wondered how Race had reacted to my letter; I wondered if he delivered my parents' letter yet, and how they took the news.

I was lost in these thoughts when Kyro sat down next to me. "Is everything OK? You seemed distracted at dinner and then slipped away once everyone else went to their rooms."

"I thought you were in your room too. How did you know I was out here?"

"Well, I did go to my room, but I'm just not ready to sleep yet. I thought I would come to see you and ask you to join me out here for a bit. It turns out you beat me to it. Unless you don't want me to join you?"

"Oh, no, please stay. I just wasn't ready to be inside for the night. I've spent so much time inside during my life. It's nice to be outside for a while."

"Are you worried about tomorrow? You know you're not alone in this mission. We're all with you. We're doing this together."

"I'm not worried." I smiled at him. "It is nice not to feel alone."

He scooted closer and gently draped his arm across my shoulders. I snuggled up to him and sighed. It was the most comfortable I had been since the night we spent at Q's hideout. I thought about that night a lot, even though nothing happened.

We sat there like that for a while, then heard a strange noise above us. It seemed to be coming from the crow's nest. Kyro jumped up, taking a defensive stance. "Go down and get the others. Hurry!" I couldn't argue with him; I was terrified of whatever was up there. I ran down the stairs to the hallway where all of our rooms were.

"Q, Mack, Gill—come quickly! Something is happening, and Kyro sent me to get you all. I think we may be under attack. Hurry!" As I yelled, I banged on their doors to wake them all up. Once I was satisfied that they were all awake and understood what I was saying, I headed back up the stairs much more carefully than I had come down them. I poked my head out the door to the deck, looking around for Kyro before creeping out silently.

The others followed me, everyone keeping low and watching for any movement. When we got to the spot where Kyro and I had been sitting, we saw him fighting off a terrifying humanoid with a six-foot wingspan. It was flying in place as it clawed and struck at Kyro, who was on his knees blocking each shot the best he could while looking for something to hide behind.

Without a sound, an arrow came from behind me and struck the flying beast. It squealed and flew off, holding the shoulder that was now home to the arrow. I turned my head in time to see Gill reloading his crossbow to fire another bolt. Before he could get the next shot off, a mighty screech came across the boat, nearly knocking us over. Q threw a flaming dagger at the beast, puncturing its other shoulder and setting it on fire.

THIRTY-ONE

Mack

AFTER Q SET THE monster on fire, it turned and appeared as if it would run away. Instead, it called out with an ear-splitting screech, dunked itself in the water to put the fire out, and circled back around. The beast had a wingspan of at least six feet, and while it resembled a woman, it was a damned ugly one. Her dark hair was stringy and matted to her head in an almost dreadlock way. Her skin had a green tint and seemed to be draped loosely over her bones, looking as though it could fall off at any moment. She wore a dirty brown dress that cascaded down, covering the monster's feet.

Gill disappeared after the first crossbow attack. I looked around for him, but I couldn't find him anywhere. The creature screeched, and there wasn't much time to worry about where Gill could have gone off to. That must have been a call for backup because within moments, and there were two more swooping down on us. One of the new ones was wearing a moldy green dress and had dirty blonde hair. The third beast had filthy russet hair, just as matted and nappy as the first two, but this was wearing a black dress.

The three ghastly women attacked us from all sides. It should have been a relatively easy fight, with five of us against three of them. With Gill taking cover, who knows where, and taking the crossbow with him, we were left at a slight disadvantage. Things got worse when Zoey was picked up by one of the nasties and dropped from about twelve feet in the air. I'm not sure if it was good or bad luck that she hit the deck instead of the water. She was knocked out, though, and I knew we'd have to protect her.

Kyro threw everything he had at them, magic and not. He tried punches and kicks but was knocked back every time. He attempted water cannons as well, and those worked a little better than physically hitting the beasts. None of his attacks were strong enough to chase the banshees off, but they were enough to keep them from attacking Zoey.

Q threw as many fireballs as she could, but these monsters could fly pretty fast. Most of the fireballs ended up either in the ocean or hitting the mast of the boat. I yelled at her, "Q, you have to focus. If you don't aim better, you'll sink the ship." If looks could kill, I would have keeled over right there. But after a minute, she nodded as though she'd thought it over and decided I might be right. Her attacks were more thought out from that point on, and she managed a better rate of shots to hits.

I swung my ax at any of the beasts that came close enough. Being the shortest, I had to climb on crates to be up high enough to pose a threat. Once I climbed up, I was able to sneak up on the blonde one. I jumped up and buried my ax in her left shoulder, pulling it down toward her chest. We landed on the deck of the boat with a thud. I stood on her stomach as she clawed at my legs. I yanked my ax free and then slammed it down into her face, cleaving her skull in two. The other two banshees screeched in pain as the blonde one died.

"They're psychically connected! They'll be weaker now with the third one dead." I made sure Q and Kyro heard me and then went on the defensive against the black-haired beast now zeroed in on me. I guess she realized I was the one who ended her friend, and she had decided to take me out. I ducked to miss her claw strike at the last possible second by doing a tuck and roll across the deck. Q shot a fireball at her, scorching her right wing and setting the hem of her dress ablaze. At first, I thought this was fantastic, and then I realized the banshee had been given another weapon to use against me. She struck out with her claws and then turned, whipping her flaming dress around. Not only did I take the nails to my chest, but then my arm was brushed by her dress, and my shirt caught fire. I tried to beat the fire out, but every time I got the flames to subside, she whipped around again, igniting a different piece of my clothing. At the rate I was going, I'd be naked and blistered all over before I got away from this monster.

Q and Kyro were working together to fight the brown-haired banshee. Q kept setting her on fire, and then Kyro would blast her with water in an attempt to drown the nasty beast. They seemed to be avoiding claw attacks and were able to keep the thing from screeching for more help. I knew that I would be able to handle this one I was fighting.

I managed to put out yet another fire on myself and then swung my ax above my head. I was trying to hit the apparition that kept attacking me. Unfortunately, I missed and sank my ax into the mast of the boat instead. As I fought to pull it back out, the demon got me across the back with her claws again. I wasn't sure how much more I could take. I was already in pain from the claw wounds on my chest and the blistering from the fire. Fortunately, the fire had cauterized the chest wounds. It hurt like a bitch, but I wasn't going to bleed to death from it. I wasn't so sure I'd be able to say the same for the wounds I'd just received on my back.

Q must have realized I was in trouble because she changed her focus from the spook that she and Kyro had been fighting to the one that was attacking me. This time, she attacked with a sword instead of her fire magic. While she sliced at the fiend, I had a chance to pull my ax free of the mast. With the beast distracted, I was able to sink my blade into her leg. As soon as I had the hag's attention, Q sliced her head off. Two down, one to go. I was reasonably sure we could do this.

Once I turned my attention to Kyro, I had my doubts. The last banshee seemed to be the leader. She was bigger and stronger than the others had been. And she was more cunning, dodging attacks and following up with claw swipes and screeches. Q took a claw strike to her right arm and doubled over from the pain of it. I had to hand it to her—as soon as she managed to rip a piece of her shirt off for a bandage, she had it wrapped up and jumped back in the fight. Watching her was impressive. She was a fierce fighter, highly skilled, and had to have been professionally trained. There was more to her than what she had been willing to share. After we survived this fight, I would have to make it a point to learn more about her. My thoughts distracted me, and I took a hit to the right side of my face, knocking me to the deck. I watched Kyro and Q beat the fiend back, giving me a chance to clear my head.

I jumped up, swinging my ax over my head. As I ran toward the demon, I let out a crazed battle cry. I knew I'd be out of reach, but I ran anyway. Kyro used his water cannon power to scoop me up and lift me to meet the beast. I sank my ax into her back, and she wailed in pain. She threw me off her, and I held tight to my ax, turning as I fell. I hit the deck with a sharp thunk, releasing my ax out of the way. As the spook charged toward me, Q unleashed a fireball at her, setting her hair and dress aflame. The banshee screeched in pain, turning toward each of us as it wailed. I rolled over and crawled to recover my ax with plans to end this beast once and for all.

THIRTY-TWO

Zoey

I REGAINED CONSCIOUSNESS JUST in time to watch as the last monster flew off again, this time dunking itself in the ocean to put out the fire before flying back over and trying another attack. This time, Mack was ready for it, swinging his ax over his head and landing it in the chest of the flying beast while releasing a guttural scream. It fell to the deck with a thud, twitching and gurgling. While the others dealt with finishing the monster off, I managed to get to my feet, realized Kyro was lying on the deck by the mast, and I raced over to him. He had been knocked out, and he was thrown into the mast of the ship.

His pulse was strong, and it appeared that he would be alright. I wasn't sure how to wake him up, though. Gill walked over, placed his hand on Kyro's chest, and muttered something. Kyro gasped, coughed, and then his eyes flew open. "What happened? Is Zoey OK? Where is that banshee?" He drifted in and out of consciousness. I wasn't sure if it was the injury or the spell that was to blame.

"Rest, brother, all is well. The monster has been dealt with. Your lady is unharmed. You almost gave your life protecting her. You need to rest now and heal." Gill spoke in such a calming tone; it would have been impossible to argue with him. Kyro didn't even try. "Take him below and put him to bed. Stay with him, but no funny business. That spell will heal him soon enough as long as he sleeps for the next eight or so hours." This was directed at me. I didn't even consider arguing. I ducked my head under Kyro's arm to help him down the stairs. Fortunately, Q grabbed his other arm and helped me carry him down.

"I'll take you to your room and get you settled, and then go get blankets from my room so I can sleep on the floor," I explained as we headed down the stairs toward his room. Once we got to his room, it seemed as though he was coming back to himself.

"Zoey, please. I'm fine. The spell will heal me. You don't need to bother."

"I won't have you argue with me, Kyro. You could have been killed just to save me. You won't be alone tonight."

"The only way I will accept this is if you sleep in the bed with me. Like at Q's. I'll be a good patient and will follow your instructions. But I won't let you sleep on my floor." As I lowered him to the bed, he reached out and grabbed me around the waist, pulling me into his lap for a kiss. The sparks as our lips touched warmed me, and I realized just how scared I was of losing him. Just as I was coming to this realization, the partially open door was pushed further open, and Gill entered with a tea tray.

"Hey! I told you no funny business! He's not going to be able to perform tonight." I jumped at Gill's voice and almost fell off Kyro's lap.

"It wasn't me! He pulled me onto his lap and started kissing me! I was trying to get him to cooperate, I promise." My words were meant to convince Gill as much as myself.

"Likely story. Just keep in mind that this particular spell will make him act a bit drunk, and he may not remember anything in the morning. Let him rest. And you," he directed his attention to Kyro, "you will stop trying to put the moves on her tonight. Or I will send her back to her room, and I'll stay with you."

Kyro laughed at the thought and then held his hands-palms up toward Gill. "Trust me, that won't be necessary. I'll behave."

"I'll just go get what I need from my room while you talk with our patient, doc," I remarked to Gill as I slipped out of the room.

I just needed a moment to collect myself. I'm not sure I could have stopped anything from happening if Gill had not interrupted. I had to get a handle on my hormones, though, for Kyro's sake. He needed to rest and heal tonight. There would be plenty of time for funny business, as Gill had called it, later.

Since I was in my room already, I grabbed my bag and then headed back to Kyro's room. Maybe we could talk to Ian for a bit since we couldn't do anything else. Perhaps he would have some insight into what the next day would bring.

When I got back to Kyro's room, Gill excused himself, but not before he reminded us to keep our clothes on and not get too excited. Kyro had to rest to heal fully. And I wanted him at his best when we finally got around to having fun.

Once Gill was gone, I asked Kyro if he needed anything, and he assured me he was fine. He looked tired but wouldn't admit it. I knew I was more tired than I realized but figured sleep would not come quickly. Kyro patted the bed beside him, asking me to climb in with him.

As I climbed into the bed, he grabbed me and flipped me over onto my back, pinning me in a passionate kiss. When he finally let me up, I swatted his arm gently and said, "You aren't supposed to do that right now! How will you ever heal if you don't rest? Gill said..." I have no idea what I was planning to say next because Kyro was kissing me again, more tenderly this time. "Mmm, this is nice, but you need to rest."

"I'm fine, I promise. Just come over here and let me kiss you," Kyro said between kissing my neck and shoulders, as I tried in vain to pull away from him. I let myself get lost in his kisses for a little while, then managed to break free and stop him.

"I want you to rest tonight. I want to be with you, but I want you to be at your best for it, and I don't want to hurt you. You promised you'd be good if I slept in here with you." I stood up as if to leave the room. I wondered if he would go along with my edict or call my bluff. I wasn't sure I could leave him if he did.

"OK, I'm sorry, I'll be good. Really. Just come, let me hold you." He sounded sincere, and the mischievous glint in his eye was gone. He looked as though the strain from being injured and healed was starting to weigh on him.

I snuggled back up against him, gave him a chaste goodnight kiss, and told him to go to sleep. He wrapped his arms around me, and within a minute, he was fast asleep. I joined him in slumber a few brief moments later. We slept for a few hours, giving ourselves time to recuperate from the earlier drama.

When he didn't wake the following day, I panicked and ran to get the others. Gill was the first one to Kyro's side, checking his pulse and breathing. "He seems to be fine. I'm not sure why he's still unconscious. Let me check my books and see what I can do." And he was gone before I could get my thoughts together.

I sat by Kyro's side for three days while Gill researched. The others came in periodically to check on his progress. We all shared defeated looks, thinking the worst. Each day he didn't wake up seemed like it was foreshadowing the end. None of us wanted to give up, but hope was waning.

Gill was right about the spell healing Kyro. We just didn't realize he'd sleep for a week while it worked.

THIRTY-THREE

Gill

I PROBABLY SHOULDN'T HAVE hidden when the banshees attacked, but I wasn't sure we could defeat them. After my first shot with the crossbow, I ducked behind some crates and then made my way below deck. I watched the fight from the safety of the doorway. I knew it wouldn't be good to be gone for the whole thing, so I made sure to come back out just as Mack killed the final beast.

I could tell Q was starting to get suspicious, especially after the jungle. I wasn't sure I could keep Kyro off my trail if she ratted me out. I could pull the best friend card, but I didn't think that would work. I'd have to lay low for a few days or weeks even to give her suspicions time to blow over. I had to find a way to throw her off. I hated to frame Mack, but I couldn't see any other way out of this.

I figured rooming with Mack was a good place to start. It would be harder for Q to find anything incriminating if she had to worry about Mack too. At first, I just did little things designed to make her wonder. But once I mastered the duplicity spell, I knew I'd be home free. It was more difficult than I had anticipated. I spent weeks laying the seeds of doubt while we traveled around searching for whatever magical trinket the wizard told Zoey he needed. The whole time, I was making it look as though Mack was interested in stealing the book.

I did my best to feign disinterest any time the group started discussing the book or the wizard. It was a practiced effort not to seem too disinterested either. I walked a very fine line. Zoey had asked Kyro and Mack to teach her to fight, and I found excuses to avoid these training sessions. I used this time to study in my room. I told them I was learning healing techniques and spells when in reality, I was practicing my duplicity spell—so it wasn't an outright lie, but rather a stretch of the truth. I searched for an invisibility spell, hoping that I wouldn't have to break into Kyro's library to get one. Sadly I had no luck with that particular endeavor.

I even planted some subliminal messages with Mack while he slept to ask Kyro about the book. After all of that, I was nearly ready to snatch it and run. I just had to find it first. Most days, Zoey either had it in her backpack on her back or hidden somewhere in her room. There was no way I could get the pack away from her without someone seeing. I needed an invisibility spell. And for that, I needed access to Kyro's library.

I had to find a time when everyone was busy and test out the duplicity spell. If I could appear to be right in front of them while I was somewhere else, I might be able to sneak into the library and steal the book that had the invisibility spell in it.

I spent a few days watching what the others did and learning their routines. I needed to make sure I was seen enough to quash any suspicions, but not so much that they knew what I was up to. I decided to follow Zoey first since I expected her to be the least likely to realize she was being followed.

Zoey began her mornings in the galley, making breakfast before heading up to the deck with a book. She would spend an hour reading before fight training. The training lasted two hours, and then they broke for lunch before switching to stamina exercises and strategy. She always helped clean up after practice, then headed down for a shower and stayed in her room until dinner. I wasn't sure what she was doing in her room, but it didn't matter. After getting her schedule down, I moved on to Q.

Q woke early and headed up to the deck every day. She walked the entire length of the boat, checking everything for who knows what. After an hour or so, she would head back down for a quick shower before breakfast. After breakfast, she would join the training but would leave a bit early to prepare lunch for everyone. Once lunch was made, she would head back up to lead the stamina exercises. After that, she would go for a swim in the ocean, unless it was storming, in which case she would go back to her room until dinner. I was more curious about what she was doing in her room. On some days, it sounded like she was talking with someone when no one was there. I didn't worry too much about it and moved onto, following my friend Mack.

Mack typically slept later, waking just in time to run to breakfast and scarf down his food. Then he would go set up the training and work with everyone until they couldn't fight anymore. After lunch, Mack would go back up on deck for stamina and strategy training. He would help Zoey clean up after the workout, and then he usually watched Q enjoy her swim. I'm sure he thought no one had noticed his apparent attraction to her. She certainly hadn't. Just before she got back on the boat, he would head down to our room, and most days, he would take a nap before going to prepare dinner. After cleaning up from dinner, he would run back to our room and shower before collapsing in his bed. His was by far the most manageable schedule to learn, in part because we shared a room. Then I moved on to Kyro.

He was the hardest to figure out because Kyro never seemed to do the same thing for two days in a row. I guessed that was life on the seas. The only consistent thing was that he woke before dawn every morning and swam in the ocean every night after everyone else was in bed. He would sometimes help with meals and clean up, sometimes he would go to the training, and other times he would lead the workouts. Sometimes he would disappear into his room after breakfast and not come out until dinner. Those days had me the most curious. I thought he was in his secret library researching that book. I had no way to confirm it, though. I would just have to be patient. Now that I knew their schedules, I just had to wait for the right moment to act. I hated waiting, but there wasn't anything I could do with Kyro passed out in his room from the banshee attack we had just survived.

While I waited, I tried my best to practice controlling my astral projection powers. I was worried because I hadn't been able to connect with my love since the dark one had accosted me. Projecting had never been my strong suit, and the only reason I could connect with the dark one so quickly was that he was always watching. There was no need to report to him unless I needed something, usually not even because he saw it all. I was beginning to wonder if the severed mental connection was my punishment that had been promised. That would be a mild punishment compared to things I'd seen his minions do to other prisoners in the weeks before Kyro and his friends came to save me. Nothing I did helped to repair the connection, so I decided that had to be it. Once I managed to complete my mission, I was sure it would be restored.

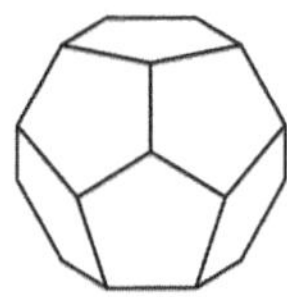

Knowing Kyro would sleep for a while because of my spell, I decided to take advantage of the break and get some sleep myself. I knew if he woke in pain, someone would come to me. The moment I drifted off, I knew it had been a bad idea. I entered the dream calm and serene and then was yanked into a dungeon where my boss's ethereal form was waiting for me. Forced astral projection was painful. This was excruciating. He stood there, made of smoke and vapor, shimmering in the light.

"Where's my book?" Straight to the point, good. I hoped this would be a short and uneventful meeting.

"I'm working on it. I need time to rest from healing my friends. I'll get it soon."

The cloud that was my captor turned red. "Why bother healing them? I'm just going to kill them after you fail me. I will have that book. Give me a reason not to kill you right now."

I was terrified but knew that we wouldn't have this conversation if he wanted me dead. He wanted me alive and scared. Both of which described my current situation perfectly. I wasn't sure what I had to bargain with, other than the fact that I had almost managed to throw suspicion onto Mack and away from myself. "I'm working on it. I'm already in with the group. I'm getting closer every day. I just had to cover my tracks from the jungle, and it's taking longer than I had planned. I'm close now."

"I've been watching you. I know you have been making it look like your friend is the guilty one. That's a good plan, and I'm interested to see how well it works. That may be the only reason I let you live. But you must pay for taking longer than we had agreed upon." He turned to the men who were guarding the door. "Bring the prisoner in."

I paled when I saw these brutes bring a humanoid with a black cloth bag over its head. I knew exactly why our connection had been severed earlier today—my love had been captured. "Please, your business is with me, not my family. Don't do this." I would beg if I had to, but I wasn't sure what I could do on this plane. I could use magic to defend us in my body, but I didn't know how that would work here. I wasn't even sure where here was, or if this was all an illusion.

"You know the price for failure. I've already given you too many chances. This one will pay for your mistakes. It's your choice how bad it gets." The smoky form nodded to the guards, and they brought the being forward. Another guard stepped up behind them, pulled out a whip, and began to dole out lashes across the back of my dear one. The cries were muffled enough that I was sure my love had been gagged.

My heart was breaking with every crack of the whip. I needed to stop this. "I'll get the book. Just stop the torture."

The cloud of fog started laughing maniacally and evaporated. "Get me the book, and we'll stop the torture. It's up to you how long this pain lasts. This is your fault."

Once the boss was gone, the guard kept cracking the whip. I couldn't take it anymore. I had to try something. I conjured up a knife and ran at the guards who were holding my love captive. "I'll save you, dear, I promise."

The moment my knife sunk into the flesh of the guard's stomach, my eyes opened, and I was back in my room, in my bed. Mack was standing over me, his eyes wide and his mouth open in shock. My hand was wet, and I was holding something. I looked down to see the knife I had conjured up in the other plane, currently in my hand and sticking in my best friend's gut.

"Oh, gods, Mack! I'm sorry, I'll fix it." His eyes met mine for a brief moment before he hit the ground. I didn't remove the knife right away, but I did let go of it as he fell. I had to make sure I hadn't hit anything important when I had stabbed him. Oh, shit. I stabbed my best friend. This situation couldn't get any worse. I had to heal Mack and get the book so that I could save my beloved. Then we would disappear, to someplace where I couldn't hurt anyone ever again.

I used my blanket to stop the flow of blood and then ran to get supplies. I knew we had a portable scanner in the medical bay. I had to get there and back quickly. I risked letting everyone know what had happened by running, but it was necessary. I had to save Mack. If it came down to it, I wasn't above lying about how he came to be stabbed in the first place.

I made it back from Sick Bay with the supplies I needed and got to work. I scanned Mack's stomach where the blade had entered and currently resided. It had nicked his intestine, but it was fixable. I would be able to heal him with my tools and magic.

I set to fix this mistake, knowing I would never get the chance to correct the other one I was currently making. After two hours and multiple moments where I thought I'd lost him, I got Mack stabilized. It didn't bother me much that he wasn't conscious. That would allow him to heal more quickly, though I worried about if there would be any lasting damage. And I wondered if they would buy the lie I had come up with about what had happened.

The way I saw it, I had at minimum until morning before I'd find out if Mack would survive the unintentional stabbing. I checked the hallway once more before crawling back into my bed and going back to sleep.

THIRTY-FOUR

Ian

IT WAS HAPPENING AGAIN. I viewed flashes of something I couldn't quite grasp. These were the worst kind of vision. At least with the others, I could prepare. If I could see the whole picture, I could figure out what it meant and deal with its consequences. With these, I only got snippets of what was going to happen, and it was never enough.

I saw a woman's hand reaching out. A ring on the index finger. Too dark to tell the type of stone in the ring. Blood...so much blood. Fire and screams. Then darkness. Flashes of red light. And the pain. The pain was unbearable. More screams...then silence. The silence was terrifying more than the screams.

Then it was over, and I woke with a start. It took me a moment to realize where I was and to keep myself from screaming. I was amazed I hadn't woken Kara with this one. Her dark brown hair was splayed across the pillow beside me, and her breathing was quiet and even, signaling that she was still asleep. I watched her for a moment as if to make sure the vision wasn't about her. Of course, there was no way to tell until the events unfolded. I would have to tuck that little bit of panic down deep, so she didn't find it. It was so hard to hide things from empaths.

The broken visions always happened when I was sleeping. There were times when I had astral projected during one of those visions and landed in the middle of the flashes. It was more agonizing from inside than out. I was relieved that I stayed inside myself this time and knew I wouldn't get back to sleep any time soon.

I decided to get up and try to work through the vision even though it was the middle of the night. I left the bed, careful not to wake Kara. At least one of us deserved a good night's sleep, and it was good that it was her, especially since she was carrying our child—just another motivator for the mission. I didn't want our daughter or son to grow up in the world the way it was now or the way it would be in the future. I had seen too many dark visions to accept what was to be without a fight. I worried that the process might kill me, leaving Kara to raise our child on her own. As fearful as I was for that to happen, I was more afraid about doing nothing.

I crept into my study, gently shut the door, and lit the candles on my desk. There was no reason for the whole neighborhood to know I couldn't sleep. I grabbed a notebook and jotted down everything I'd seen. Then I started trying to make sense of it. It was too dark to know whose hand it was or whose blood. I even sketched out the images, thinking that seeing the details would make it easier to figure out. Once I had written down everything I could remember and had drawn out all the images, I sat back in my chair and looked over it all.

When Kara walked in with a fresh cup of coffee hours later, I was still sitting there, pondering what it all could mean. "Oh, love, you didn't have to make coffee for me. I know how it turns your stomach lately. But thank you." I stood and kissed her as I took the cup from her hand.

"It does, but I won't let that stop me from taking care of you. The gods know you need me. If it weren't for me, you wouldn't stop long enough to eat. And you know it." She wasn't wrong. If she weren't interrupting me for meals or breaks, I would probably work myself to death trying to figure all of this out.

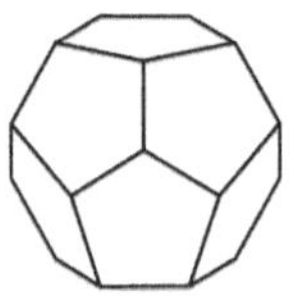

After we ordered in for breakfast, Kara teleported to her job at the magic school. She was a counselor there and took great pride in helping shape the youth. I had no doubt they were kinder and more brilliant for having known her. She was the one person who understood my need to remain at home, where the Order couldn't find me. She even wore a cloaking charm when she left to make sure they couldn't track her as well.

Once she left, I got back to my research. I had so many books to read and so little time. As I read through text after text, I began to feel strange, as though I was going to pass out. I knew from experience that this was one of the ways a vision began. I laid on the floor to keep from harming myself, as this type of vision appeared to be very much like a seizure. I barely had time to lower myself out of the chair before it took me.

I paid careful attention to each detail revealed in that vision, as I would need to relay it to Zoey later. This one was a doozy. Someone on the boat was a spy for the Order. They were trying to steal the book. And if I didn't do something, this vision showed they would succeed. Once the image subsided, I rested for a moment and then grabbed the journal to see if I could get Zoey's attention.

I had no idea if time flowed in the same way in the future or not, but I was hopeful. I tried for hours to get Zoey to open the book and talk to me with no success. I realized I would have to keep trying intermittently not to miss my chance to warn her. I just hoped I wasn't already too late. My biggest regret was that I didn't have a name to give her. Things would have been so much easier if I had seen who it was.

THIRTY-FIVE

Zoey

WITH KYRO SLEEPING BECAUSE of Gill's spell, I spent a lot of time in his room. I probably could have used that time researching with Ian or preparing for whatever was going to come next. Thoughts of losing Kyro so soon kept me from focusing on anything but keeping him comfortable. And I was exhausted from worrying. It had already been a week since the attack, and he hadn't woken yet. I was surprised I was sleeping at all.

I woke in the morning to an empty bed. Kyro's spot was still warm so that he couldn't be far. I knew Gill would be checking on him, so I took a moment to peruse the book for helpful information before discussing our plan with the others.

As I pulled the book from my bag, it began to vibrate as it had when I first found it. I took that as a sign that Ian wanted to talk to me. I climbed back into the bed with the book and opened it in front of me. The blank pages glowed as Ian's words appeared.

Zoey, I'm so glad you're here. I've been trying to get your attention. I had a vision of you being attacked and was worried something had happened. Are you alone? Can we talk without anyone else hearing or seeing?

"Yes, I am alone right now. But we were attacked last night by something Kyro called banshees...they were terrifying, bony, and pale, with wings that looked to be made of bones and skin. They were powerful, too; one almost killed Kyro. But it's alright because Gill healed him. And Mack helped Q kill the monster."

Oh, I truly hope that is what my vision warned of; otherwise, I fear you're in grave danger from within your vessel. Sadly, this vision wasn't very clear or specific, but I felt the threat so vividly. I am not sure where the danger lies, but I fear you cannot trust any of your companions. Any one of them could be a spy for the Order, or worse, a warlock out for themselves. Please promise me you will be careful and take care with whom you share the book.

"Oh! That is a scary thought. Could one of my new friends truly be an enemy? I know I've been quick to trust in the past, but I think my judgment is generally good. How will I know if it is one of them? Can you tell me more about the Order?"

I fear there isn't time. But I will try to explain quickly. The Order was created as a way to assist those with magic in the beginning. If Ed and I had known just how far they would take it, we never would have chartered the organization. It was meant to keep magic safe, not steal it. But, as happens on occasion, one with great power came to hold the Chairman's seat in the Order, and things changed. The Order became about collecting energy and using it to further the Chairman's agenda. I don't know much else, but I will research and let you know the next time we talk. Please visit me regularly, so I know you are safe. I will pass along any information I can find.

After assuring Ian that I would take care and also that I would check in more often, I put the book back in my bag and hid my bag in Kyro's room. I didn't think anyone would look for it there. I wasn't sure if I believed Ian's warning about my new friends, but I wasn't going to take any chances. I didn't know enough about any of them just to hand over the book.

I went to the galley to see if anyone else was having breakfast and to get something to eat myself. I thought it was still early, but no one was around. I helped myself to some fruit and juice and then decided to check up on deck. When I stepped out into the fresh air, I could hear voices. I decided to approach quietly and see what I could hear.

"I just think it would be safer for all of us if we knew where the book is and what's in it. It's easier to protect something if we all know what we're protecting. I don't understand why you can't see that. Just let me ask Zoey. I'm sure she won't mind sharing the book with the rest of us." Mack sounded pretty determined to get his hands on the book. Maybe he was the spy. I would have to keep an eye on him.

"Look, I already told Gill, and now I'm telling you. You can either trust me or not. If you're not going to trust me, though, why did you choose to come with us? Plain and simple, it's Zoey's place to decide who can interact with the book. I'm not going to ask her, and neither are you. If there's something we need to see, she'll show us. Please drop it, Mack. I'm not going to budge on this one." Kyro was equally insistent that they were not going to get the book.

"I'm just trying to help. I trust you and her. For real, Ky. I just want to make sure it stays safe."

I felt lousy eavesdropping on Kyro's conversation with his friend, but I was glad to have a little more knowledge about Mack and Gill's intentions. I made a big show of walking around the corner, making sure to make enough noise that they knew I was coming, but not so much to be suspicious.

"Good morning, Zoey. I trust you slept well? Or did our boy's snores keep you from getting enough rest?"

"I slept just fine, Mack; thank you for asking. Am I interrupting something?"

"No, Mack and I were just discussing the book." At least I could trust Kyro to be open with me. "Mack and Gill think we should all have access, and I disagree. I have explained both that you have been selected as the chosen one, and if you choose to share the book, you will. No one is going to guilt or force you to let them see it."

"Thank you, Kyro. That means a lot to me." It did. It seemed like just when I thought I couldn't like him more, he did or said something like this, and I felt myself on the verge of falling in love with him. "I'm not trying to keep anything from anyone; I'm just not sure it's safe for everyone to have full access to it. I have to protect Ian and make sure we can complete the mission."

"Speaking of the mission, I probably need to get started on weapons for the next part. I know we had planned a briefing this afternoon. As long as we're still on for that, I'll see you both then." And with that, Mack walked off in a huff.

"Is he OK?" I asked Kyro casually. There were so many other things I wanted to ask. Like, is either of your friends a secret member of an even more secret organization hellbent on stealing the book from me? But I figured this was neither the place nor the time for that particular conversation. I was not planning to accuse anyone without some form of proof. And I didn't feel that Ian having an unclear vision paired with Kyro's conversations was enough proof. I would just have to keep my eyes and ears open. Hopefully, I would be able to flush out the spy before they could get the book.

"He's just a moody dwarf. He likes to get his way and is probably pissed that you showed up before he could try and talk me into strong-arming you into letting him see the book. I just don't think the time is right for everyone to be gathered around for storytime. I'm not even sure that I completely trust Ian yet. So far, he's been right about what he's told us, but I have a gut feeling that he's not telling us everything." Kyro stepped closer and leaned down, kissing me on the cheek. "But don't worry about that right now. It's all going to work out."

"I know it will. It's just a lot to take in. What do you think Gill and Mack want with the book?"

Kyro looked out at the ocean for a moment and then turned back to me. "I'm not sure what either of them would wish to gain by having access to it. I just don't think it's a good idea to be parading it around. Unless you disagree?"

"Oh, no, I think you're right. Without knowing why they want the book, I don't feel right about sharing it with anyone besides you."

"Now that the matter is settled let's move onto planning for the next mission. You should get your notes so we can go over them and figure out how to explain what we're doing and what we're looking for to the others."

Over the next few days, we sailed and talked about the mission. We were looking for an enchanted sword that was somewhere in the area of Japan. Ian wasn't exactly sure where, but its last known whereabouts were in a small town on the island's coast. We still had about a week until we would arrive, and I still wasn't any closer to figuring out if someone was a spy or not. If anything, I was becoming more paranoid about it and suspected everyone at one time or another.

THIRTY-SIX

Kyro

We had been sailing for a while, searching for these pearls and the dodecahedron Ian had told Zoey we needed so we could fix the world. As much as I wanted to help Zoey, I wasn't sure I trusted Ian. He wanted us to find an enchanted dodecahedron and three magical pearls. He claimed to have limited knowledge of their locations, but I wasn't buying it. He had sent her to me for a reason. I was confident he knew my secret, but neither of us had acknowledged it. But since I had one of the pearls, I was betting I knew precisely why I was chosen for this mission.

Maybe I was wrong, and he didn't know yet that I had it, but I was convinced that Ian would be plotting to steal the pearl from me the second he found out. Because of this, I kept it locked up in a hidden safe inside my quarters on the boat. No one knew I had it, not even Mack or Gill. I would wait until we had the other three pieces of the puzzle before revealing this to the others. Then I would make sure to tell them all at the same time so the others could see just how crooked Ian was. Unless I was wrong, and he honestly did just want to save the world.

But I wasn't sure what that would mean for me. Would I lose my powers and just be a regular man after magic was tamed again? Would the world be the way my mother had wanted it? I wasn't sure that I liked that. The only thing I was sure of was that I wanted to end up with Zoey when all of this was over. She was terrific and seemed to be opening up more every day. She was coming out of her shell. We didn't talk about our families, so that wasn't an issue.

We spent our days hunting for pearls and our evenings researching their powers. Through all this, I was trying to figure out precisely what Ian was planning. So far, I had hit a dead end. I couldn't find anything that indicated he had an ulterior motive, though I had a feeling there was something he wasn't telling us after a hard morning of training while en route to the next clue; I excused myself to take a shower.

Once I was certain no one had followed me, I locked my door and pulled the pearl from its hiding place. Holding it in my hand, I could feel the power emanating from it. I wasn't sure precisely what ability this one had, but I knew it was one of three—it could either control time, control the weather, or reveal the holder's deepest desires and the path to obtain them. I wondered how this would work with the dodecahedron and where we would find that and the other two pearls.

The pearl in my hand began to glow slightly and became warm against my skin. I stared in astonishment as it projected a scene on the wall in front of me. It appeared as though I had the pearl of desire. Currently, it was showing me my deepest desire, projected on my wall. The scene showed a tiny cottage, with Zoey standing on the porch and three small children playing in the yard. That seemed pretty accurate to me. I would love for this to end that way. Now I just had to figure out how to make that happen.

I put the pearl back in its hiding place and took my shower. We had a few quiet days lately, and I was sure that wouldn't last. Ian had warned us that the Order would come for the book. We'd been training so we would be ready for them. I wasn't sure that we were. As I stepped out of the shower, I heard a commotion on deck. I threw on a pair of pants and ran up the stairs to see what was going on. Pirates had boarded the boat. The others were defending the entrances that led below the deck. Or at least most of them were—I didn't see Gill. It became apparent that these were no ordinary pirates.

They carried magic-infused swords and seemed impossible to defeat. I shot blasts of water at two of them, knocking them off the side of the boat, but they climbed back up and kept coming at me. Q was off to my left, shooting fireballs at these pirates as they dodged or ran from her. Mack was back to back with Zoey, working together to push three of the pirates back. I had no idea where Gill was and didn't have time to look for him.

There was eight pirates total, and I didn't see a way for us to win against their magic weapons. Q was chasing three of them around the boat deck with fireballs while Mack and Zoey appeared to be getting the upper hand finally. That left the final two for me to defeat. Since magic didn't seem to be helping, I grabbed a sword and attacked. They were skilled with blades. This fight wasn't going to be as easy as I had hoped. It looked as though we might lose control of the boat to these guys with everyone tied up.

I couldn't let that happen. I blasted the guy on my left as I swung at the one on my right. I barely managed to get past his block and sliced his sword arm off at the wrist. I expected there to be quite a bit of blood, but there was none. These were not human pirates. I wasn't sure what they were. The guy who had just lost his hand was distracted enough that I could get a few more hits in. Before he could recover, I had sliced him in half and threw him overboard. Then I turned to the other one.

As I did, I noticed two of the guys Q had been chasing was reduced to ash on the deck, and one of the guys Mack and Zoey had been fighting was missing as well. It was a bit comforting to know that we had cut their numbers in half within just a few minutes. The last four guys weren't giving up, and we were all beginning to show our exhaustion. I felt like we were fighting a losing battle. It was as though some outside force was sapping our energy. Mack and Zoey managed to take out one more of the guys attacking them, making it a four-to-three fight. I liked the odds shift, but without enough energy to lift my sword, it wasn't going to help much.

I kept scanning the boat for any sign of what was siphoning our energy. My friends appeared to be wearing down as well. It was becoming more of a struggle to stay on my feet and to keep my sword moving. Just as I was about to give up, an arrow sailed over my head and knocked the sword from the hand of the pirate I was fighting. Suddenly I felt a surge of strength and cleaved him in two, pushing the body over the edge of the boat before moving on to help my friends.

I looked over my shoulder to see where the arrow had originated, though I was sure I knew. Gill was standing in the crow's nest with his bow and a quiver of arrows. Well, at least I didn't have to wonder where he was anymore. He nodded to me as he aimed again. If we could separate these pirates from their weapons, we might be able to win. Mack must have seen what happened because he decided to see if wielding the pirates' weapons would give us an advantage.

The moment he touched the sword, he collapsed onto the deck and passed out. Zoey paused for a moment to check on him and then yelled, "He's alive. Don't touch the swords!" Q and I both nodded in response as Zoey kicked the sword from Mack's hand. We would have to protect him and keep these pirates from knocking us out and taking over the boat. Gill kept launching arrows at the swords, and the rest of us refocused our efforts on knocking the blades away from us.

Q blasted one of the pirates with a fireball, and I sliced through him with my sword as Zoey kept the other two busy. With four of us and two of them left, defeating them should have been easy. Gill managed a headshot, and one went down.

I kicked the sword overboard and focused on the last pirate. He got past me and sliced Q's left arm with his sword. She instantly fell to the ground, unconscious. The final pirate got cocky and decided to take on both Zoey and me at the same time. While we had him distracted, Gill was able to land another kill shot. With all the pirates killed, Zoey and I collapsed onto the deck, breathing hard and exhausted. That fight seemed to last forever.

Gill climbed down from the crow's nest and walked over to where Zoey and I lay on the deck. As he walked, he kicked deceased pirate parts off the edge of the boat. Once Gill made it to where we were, he checked on Mack and then Q. Satisfied that they would survive, he began a healing ritual that would help us regain the strength that had been stolen from us. After a few minutes, Zoey and I were feeling more like ourselves. The spell seemed to help Q and Mack as well. Once it was cast, they appeared to be sleeping peacefully instead of the fitful, cursed way they had been.

Gill and I carried Mack down to his bunk and settled him in for the night. I didn't like leaving Zoey up on deck by herself, but she had assured me it would be fine. She waited with Q until I came back to get her. We tucked her into bed next and then got ourselves settled in for a rest. We all knew that the Chairman had sent the undead pirates, but none of us knew how or exactly why. It didn't seem as though they had the brain capacity to steal the book, so that it couldn't have been that. It must have been to disable us so someone else could come for the book. With any luck, everyone would be feeling normal when we woke the following day.

THIrTY-seven

Kyro

EVERYTHING SEEMED TO BE going well. We'd had a few uneventful days. I should have been on guard or skeptical because of that, but I wasn't. Things were looking up. Since the

banshee attack and even since the pirate attack, we had been training daily at Mack's insistence. We had to learn how to protect ourselves without magic. It was a good idea, and I kicked myself for not thinking of it first. After training, we would all split off and go our separate ways to relax or partake in our hobbies before beginning meal prep and sailing responsibilities.

Zoey had gone to take a long bath, so I was sitting alone, hanging my feet over the side of the boat, when Q approached me from behind. "We need to talk."

I almost launched myself off the side of the boat. "Oh, Q. I didn't see you there. You startled me. What's up?"

She cocked an eyebrow at me expectantly. "You wanna play it that way? Fine. I know. About your mother."

My jaw dropped. My mother wasn't something I discussed, and as far as I knew, the only people on the boat who knew anything about it were Mack and Gill. Both of them had been sworn to secrecy, so I knew they hadn't talked. The pain was unbearable. "What are you talking about?" I hoped she was bluffing, but from what I knew about her so far, she wasn't.

"I know she's with the Order. What I don't know is why you haven't bothered to tell us all. Or do the others already know?" She stared at me blankly, waiting for a response.

"My mother was with the Order, but at some point, after she abandoned me and then tried to have me killed, they turned on her and killed her. So I guess you don't know as much as you thought. Yes, the guys know, but Zoey doesn't. As for not telling you, I'm sure there are things you haven't told the rest of us either. So don't get all high and mighty with me. It's none of your business. So drop it." With that, I stood up, turned, and walked away.

Before I got out of earshot, I heard her say, "She's not dead. It was faked. I'm sorry I upset you, but I had to know if you were working with her against us." She turned and walked away as though she hadn't just dropped a life-altering truth bomb on me. I didn't stop her. I wanted to be alone with my thoughts. I had to find a way to confirm what she had told me. I headed down to my cabin. I gathered the supplies I would need and then proceeded to call Ari in the scrying bowl.

"Kyro! What a surprise!" Ari seemed genuinely delighted to see me.

"Ari, I have questions, and I need definitive answers." I made sure my voice sounded stern, and I blocked all emotion from seeping through.

"What is it, Kyro? Are you OK?" She paused a moment, and I watched her eyes become guarded. "So you found out. I wondered how long it would take you."

For the second time tonight, my jaw dropped. "So it's true? She's alive? And you knew? How could you know and not tell me?" I was pissed and made sure she knew it.

"Kyro, please, calm down. You know why I didn't tell you. I told your father, and he swore me to secrecy. I tried to talk him out of it, but he said you'd been through too much already. I told him you'd discover the truth. Please listen to me." I couldn't stand there any longer. I had to leave, though I could have just broken the connection. I stormed out the door, up onto the deck, and jumped into the water. I started swimming and didn't look back. At first, I swam as hard and fast as possible to distance myself from the truth. After a couple of hours, I slowed down and swam more leisurely, trying to clear my head.

I was so pissed. My mother was alive. And my father knew but didn't want me to find out. A part of me understood why, but I would never tell him that. Even more hurtful was that she had faked her death. Why? What could she have gained by doing that? Was she planning to come after me again? I started to panic. What if she attacked the boat while I was gone? I wouldn't live with myself if something happened to Zoey or the others. But I couldn't go back yet. I needed answers.

It didn't matter where I was; I could always find my home. There was something about being half fish, after all. I knew it would offend the old man if he knew I thought about it that way, which is probably why I did. We'd never been particularly close, but I had to give him credit; he tried more with me than most of his other children. It helped that his wife loved me as though I was her son, but that was probably because I had always shown her more respect than he did. What kind of man ran around having affairs behind his wife's back just because he was a god? Our difference of opinion on that matter may have had a little something to do with our issues. I knew I would have to talk to him, though.

Maybe I would start with my stepmother, Amphitrite, instead of going straight to the old man. Amphi had always told me the truth, and I knew she would steer me in the right direction. Besides, I already knew my father wouldn't be there. He rarely spent time with her when there wasn't a festival or official business. I found her in her garden. Her silver hair glistened in the moonlight, and her tail was the palest shade of blue. She was beauty and love incarnated. She turned to me with her arms out the second she sensed me. "Come, child, Mama is here." I let myself collapse into her embrace. "It's OK; I'm here. Please tell me what troubles you, though I'm certain I already know. I'm sure it's the reason your father has gone out. He's looking for you." She hugged me and patted my back, the way my mother did when I was a small child.

I let myself break down while I was in her arms. Crying wasn't something I did, but at that moment, I let it all out. When I was finished, I spoke. "So you knew too?" She kissed my cheek. "Oh, sweet boy. I wanted to tell you, but you know how your father is. He was only trying to protect you."

I nodded. "I know. Please don't tell him that. But it still hurts that other people knew, and it was kept from me."

She hugged me again before releasing me. "I know it hurts. Her behavior has hurt me for years. But there's nothing we can do about it now. I was hoping that we'd be done with all this when you didn't hear from her right away. I wanted her to stay gone and for you to move on with your life."

"Why did she change?" I didn't expect Amphi to have the answer, but I had to ask.

"I don't know, dear. I think part of it was jealousy. Your mother expected me to hate you, but from the moment I saw your sweet face, I loved you as my own child." It didn't surprise me. "I didn't want to tell you this, but I feel like you have a right to know." It was never good when a talk started that way. Amphi motioned for me to sit by her on a bench in the garden.

"The summer when your father gave you the gift of land and sea, your mother had a fit at first. She was so angry that I would get to spend time with you when she wasn't there. All our visits had been supervised to that point; you see. She was worried that you would love me more than you did her. I tried to comfort her and explain that a child's love for his mother would never be replaced, but she would not have it." Amphi shook her head gently and closed her pale blue eyes against the tears that were forming.

"She called me to come to her while you were with us. She offered to give you to me, like my own, in exchange for power. She wanted to trade her flesh and blood for magical abilities. As much as I loved you then and love you now, I refused. I would not give her powers for any price. It was shortly after that day that she seemed to change." The tears began to escape her eyes and run down her cheeks.

"So when she decided to try to strip me of my powers, that was just a way for her to try to gain them for herself?" Amphi nodded, and I joined her in crying tears of sadness for my mother.

"There's no way to know what happened to her, but once she got mixed up with the Order, I knew there was no way to bring her back. Your father sent guards to try. She refused and even trapped a couple of them. The whole thing has been tragic and breaks my heart."

Amphi encouraged me to spend the night and had a guest room made up for me. I still hadn't seen my father, but that was fine by me. I wasn't sure what I would do the next day, but I wasn't ready to go back just yet. As I was settling in for the night, Amphi came in. "I brought you something to eat. And there's something else." I paused and looked up at her from where I was sitting. "You are so much better than her. You always have been. Don't ever doubt that, child. Your light shines so brightly. Don't let her snuff that out." She kissed my cheek and left.

I went out to see her in her garden in the morning. My father was with her. I watched from outside the gate as she excused herself to allow us privacy to talk. Poseidon was a hulk of a man, or merman, as the case may be. His white hair was full and thick, falling almost to his waist. His mustache and beard were just as magnificent, and the pale white of them made his tanned skin even more pronounced. He appeared to be maybe fifty at the most, though we all knew he was quite a bit older than that. He had a chest and arms that were well-toned and may have been why most mermen went shirtless. It was easy to see why Amphi fell for him and why so many human women threw themselves at him.

No matter how gorgeous my father was, I still thought he should have been faithful to her. She was his wife, after all. I realized it was a stupid thought because if he had been, I wouldn't exist. But if I didn't exist, my mother would have followed a different path, and Amphi might have been happier. There was no going back to change the past now, so we would just have to move forward the best we could. Right now, that meant talking to my father as his wife had advised. I had promised her I'd keep an open mind no matter how angry I was.

I knew he was there the moment I walked up to the garden. There was no hiding it. We seemed to have the ability to sense each other. I was certain Amphi had called him to come to talk to me last night. She was insistent that we get everything out in the open and move forward. I wasn't sure that was possible but decided I would try for her sake. I had stopped just inside the gate and was considering walking away when he walked over. I turned to face him as he approached.

"Son. I've been looking everywhere for you. Are you OK?" I scoffed at his question. Then he did something unexpected. He stepped forward and pulled me into a hug—not a half hug or a side hug, but—a full-on bear hug. I was caught off guard, and my arms wrapped around him on their own. I rested my forehead on his chest, and the tears came again. I ducked my head so he couldn't see them. I hated looking weak in front of him.

"It's OK to cry, Son. There's no shame in emotion. I'm sorry I made you feel as though there was." I looked up at him and saw the tears in his eyes. "I'm sorry, my boy, I should have told you. But you were so much better off with her dead. The light had just started coming back in your eyes. I think that has something to do with your lady. But now I fear I've lost you forever."

His words caught me off guard more than the hug had. Did he mean what he was saying? "I know this isn't the time to go into all of this, but I hope that someday you will come to visit me and we can have this talk. For now, you need to get back to your lady and her quest. Just know that I will be here for you, and I will do my best to help in any way I am able." He gathered me into his arms once more for a hug and then shooed me off before I could say anything in response. I didn't get to speak a single word in that entire conversation, but it felt like we had begun to mend things.

Amphi was waiting for me by the gate as I swam away from my father. "I told you that you'd feel better after you talked to him." She pulled me into a hug, and I kissed her cheek.

"Thank you. For everything. I love you, Mama." Her eyes misted over as she touched my cheek. I gathered the bag of supplies she had brought for me and headed back to my boat and friends. I'd only been gone a few days, but it already seemed like too long.

THIRTY-EIGHT

Mack

WE TRAINED HARD FOR days while Kyro went wherever it was he had run off to. Nobody seemed to know. I suspected that Q had an idea of why he had taken off, even though she denied it. I cornered her after training the day after Kyro disappeared. "I think you know something about this, and you're just not talking. That looks mighty suspect on your part."

She looked down at me with disdain. "I told you and everyone else this morning, I don't know anything about Kyro leaving." I squinted up at her, considering that response.

"How are you so calm then? How do you not think something has happened? What if he's been taken?"

She looked unconcerned. "I don't think he's been taken. Kyro can protect himself. I think he took off. Maybe he's working with the Order, and he left to check-in. We don't know."

I glared at her. "You may not know, but I damn well do—Kyro would never work for them. He's an honest man, and I'll not be letting you say any different. So you can tell me what you know, or you can get off at the next stop."

She looked shocked at my statement. "What makes you so sure I know something?"

"Because I'm better at reading people than Zoey is. And you've done pretty well trying to avoid the question every time it gets asked. Not to mention, you've been pretty successful at avoiding us all day today. It comes across very suspicious." I wasn't buying her lies. I just wasn't sure I could make her talk without using force. And I'd been raised better than that.

"I don't know anything more about Kyro leaving than you do. I told you what I think happened. I think he's a double agent, and he's luring us into a trap. Just because you're too naive to see it doesn't make me guilty of anything." She crossed her arms over her chest and stuck her nose in the air haughtily.

"Have it your way, woman...you can get off the boat now if you're just after arguing. I'll have answers, or you'll swim." I wasn't sure that I'd throw her overboard, but if she believed me, it might help my cause. I needed answers. I needed to know what had happened.

"I told you, I don't know anything." She seemed determined to keep what she knew to herself. And I was determined to get it out of her. As I took a step toward her, she took a step back.

"If you aren't here to help us, then you have to go." I wasn't backing down. I took another step toward her, and she stepped back again. She hesitated and then pulled me behind some crates for privacy. "Fine, but first," she spoke softly, "tell me, just how well do you know him?"

I stepped up onto a crate before I answered. I wanted to be in her face for this argument. "I've known Kyro for more than half my life. I know him better than anyone. We're like brothers. Why? I knew you knew something. Stop beating around the bush and just tell me already." I glared up at her. Her expression changed slightly. Her eyes seemed to soften for a moment in what might have been sadness or regret, and then the cold was back.

"What do you know about his mother?" she asked. Suddenly my feet were the most exciting things I'd ever seen. I couldn't look away from them. They were so fascinating that I couldn't look away from them. My eyes refused to meet her gaze.

"Shannon's dead." I wouldn't say anything else. I couldn't. The lump forming in my throat prevented it.

"But she didn't die. And my intel says she works for the Order. Did you know?" Now, who was asking the questions?

My head snapped up, and my eyes were huge as they met hers. "How did you find out about that? He doesn't talk about her since she tried to kill him. He's mortified that she's in league with those people. But she's dead. We saw it happen."

She shook her head slowly. "I have my ways of knowing. She's not dead. I can assure you."

I didn't understand.

"What does any of this have to do with Kyro disappearing? Wait—did you tell him? Did you tell him that his mother isn't dead? That the woman who tried to have him killed is still out there, and he's not safe like he thought?"

She nodded, and for the first time, her face looked guilty. "I had to know if Kyro was working with her. I didn't know that he thought she was dead. And I had no idea that he would run off when I brought the subject up."

"Of course, he's not working with her. Even if he'd wanted to, she'd have nothing to do with him. It's been that way for years. Did you not hear me say she tried to have him killed? He had to be shocked by the news since he was convinced that he had watched her die. Hell, I'm shocked by the news. How could we have known that she didn't die that day? What else do you know?" I pressed for answers and stared her down while she processed the questions.

"I heard you—I just wasn't convinced that she tried to kill him. He told me that much himself. I figured he was in on it, especially since he swore to me that she was dead. But I know that the Order faked her death. They blew her house up but snuck her out a trap door in the floor, so she didn't even get hurt."

I shook my head as I paced back and forth across the tops of the crates. At least now I knew why Kyro had left. I just didn't know where he had gone. This news was bad, so very bad. I stopped and grabbed her by the collar. Our faces were so close that I could have captured her full lips with my own. This wasn't the time for those thoughts, so I pushed it away and pressed her harder. "Do you even understand what you've done? Do you even care?"

"I know you have more questions, and I understand that you don't trust me. I need you to know that if I could tell you more, I would. I cannot answer anything else. I can't tell you anything more about how I got my intel. Just know that I'm here to help, and I have connections that we can call on if we need to." I knew she had secrets and planned to keep an eye on her, but I couldn't find a way to force it out of her. She excused herself from my company and left me standing there dumbfounded. I didn't even try to stop her.

I would have to be content with knowing that she'd help when and how she could. And I would have to be the one to take care of things until Kyro returned if Kyro returned. News of his mother may have broken him. I decided we would have to train even harder.

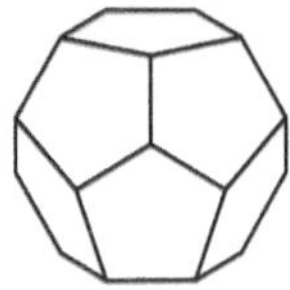

Zoey sought me out a bit later. "Mack, do you know where Kyro went or when he will be back?" Her face was stricken with concern.

"I know you're worried, lass, but our boy can take care of himself. I don't know where he's gone off to or when he's coming back. But I do know that if I had a lass as pretty as you waiting for me, I wouldn't stay gone long. That's for sure."

She blushed but seemed relieved that I wasn't worried. I was terrified but chose to hide that from everyone. With any luck, Kyro would be back by nightfall. I would have to arrange watches to be sure we saw him if he did come back in the middle of the night. I went to see if Gill had made any progress with his scrying spell after I had put Zoey's mind at ease. It broke my heart to see her in pain.

Kyro slipped back onto the boat when he thought none of us was looking. I didn't confront him about it since I knew why he'd left. From the look on his face, I was certain I knew where he'd been. His step-mother had always been able to calm the storm inside of him. Now I just had to distract everyone else until he was ready to talk.

I didn't have to distract them for long. He showed up at training bright and early the following day, pushing us to keep working. He still wasn't ready to talk yet, so I waited.

THIRTY-NINE

Zoey

WE DECIDED IT WOULD be a good idea to continue to practice fighting even while Kyro was gone since most of us were
not very skilled. Most likely, we would have to fight our way

through most of these missions to find the items Ian needed to fix his past mistakes. Since Kyro came back, he was even more determined for us to be in top fighting form, though he didn't want to discuss precisely why. Our training sessions kept getting more challenging, though. I was headed back to my room to clean up and rest after a tough workout session with Mack when I caught Q leaving my room.

"Oh, good, there you are," she sighed.

"What were you doing in my room?" I wasn't sure I could take her on if she decided to fight me, but I wasn't going to back down if she turned out to be the spy.

"I was looking for you. There's something we need to talk about." She didn't seem upset that she had been caught and appeared genuinely relieved to have run into me.

"What's up?" I had so many more questions for her, but I figured I should start with the easiest to answer first.

"Can we go inside and talk? I don't want to have this conversation out here where anyone could hear." She glanced around nervously, as though she suspected someone was listening.

"OK, come on in. We can talk about whatever is on your mind." I opened the door and led the way in.

We sat at the small table on the left side of the room, opposite the bed. I waited for Q to settle in and start talking.

"I think we have a spy on board." Q's eyes scanned my face as if looking for answers.

"What makes you say that?" I was shocked to hear this from her. It would be a bold move for the spy to approach me and declare their existence. This statement both confused and comforted me. Perhaps she was trustworthy after all.

"Well, I can't say for sure, but I've heard hushed conversations about the book, and it sounded like someone was planning to take it. I didn't see who was talking, and I'm not familiar enough with everyone's voices to know for sure who it was. I'm not even sure who he was talking with."

"I see. What did they say?" I was trying to play it cool and not show that I had already suspected as much.

"I didn't get enough to know. Something about midnight tonight and having to get the book before a rendezvous tomorrow when we dock the boat."

She seemed sincere, but I just didn't know who to trust. There were only five of us on the boat, so if it wasn't me, and it wasn't her that just left Kyro, Gill, and Mack. I couldn't believe Kyro would betray me like that, so that left Gill and Mack. There were no other people on the boat. It didn't make sense that anyone else could be involved. I had to find out what their plan was so that I could stop them.

"Then I guess I'll have to make sure the book is somewhere safe tonight."

"I can hide it for you if you'd like. I won't tell the guys; it'll just be a secret between us."

I found it interesting that she would come in here and tell me someone wanted to steal the book and then suddenly offer to keep it safe for me. At that moment, I honestly didn't feel like I could trust her either. But I couldn't tell her that. I had to come up with a plan to draw out the spy. I just needed to buy myself some time to set it up.

"That would be great. I can't give it to you right now, because I need it for some work I have to do. But come back tonight, and I will give it to you for safekeeping." I hoped my years spent watching Race lie to his parents allowed me to pick up some of his skill. I needed her to believe me for my plan to work.

"Sounds good. I'll come back tonight after everyone is turned in for the night." And with that, she left the room.

Once I was sure she was gone, I turned the lock on the door and tugged the handle to make sure I was locked inside. The door didn't budge, so I pulled out the book and asked Ian what he thought about the conversation I just had with Q. Then I explained my plan for that night and asked for his advice on it. He agreed that it might be our best shot to discover who the spy was and what they wanted with the book.

"Have you had any more visions about who it may be?"

I have not. However, I have had visions of Kyro helping us reach the dodeca. I feel very strongly that he is not the spy. As for the others, I have tried meditating on their intentions given the details you have provided me with, and I'm just not getting anything helpful. Have you had any luck counter-spying?

"Not really. I've made myself so paranoid that I don't know if I can trust myself anymore. But I am bound to protect the book. I won't let a spy take it."

You should let Kyro in on your plan and ask for his assistance. I genuinely feel that we can trust him on this. I have not seen the others in my visions of the future, so I cannot say if any of them is trustworthy, but Kyro has been in several. Please keep the book with you until you've talked to him. I fear it is the only way to keep our connection safe.

"I shall not fail you, friend. We will fix this. But for now, I must find Kyro." I closed the book and put it in my bag. I would just have to keep my bag on me the rest of the day and keep an eagle eye out for anyone being overly interested in it.

I found Kyro in his room, resting after his workout session with Gill. He was trying to learn how to channel his water abilities to help us best. We were confident there would be more monsters to fight. It was just a matter of how long before the next battle.

"Kyro? Do you have a moment? There's something I need to discuss with you."

He seemed to notice my hesitation. "Of course, Zoey, anything for you. What do you wish to discuss?"

I walked in, closing and securing the door behind me. If anyone had seen me come in and tried to follow, they might think we were fooling around, but that was the least of my worries. "This isn't easy to say..."

"Is something wrong? Did something happen? Are you alright? Is the book safe?"

"Well, I had a visitor after my workout. And I have to tell you something I've been keeping to myself. I promise I wasn't trying to keep things from you; I just didn't want to say anything until I had proof."

"Zoey, what are you talking about? Proof of what?"

"Ian thinks there is a spy among us, and I agree with him, though neither of us can figure out who it is."

I proceeded to tell him about the strange things I had heard over the past few days and of my visit from Q. I told him about Ian's warning that someone was a spy and of all the things that made me suspicious of his friends as well as Q. His face knotted up with concern.

"So you see, Kyro, I have no idea which one is the spy, but they all want the book. I have to set a trap to discover who it is. I knew I couldn't do it without you, but I didn't want to accuse your lifelong friends unless I had proof." I waited, wringing my hands, for him to process all that I had just told him.

"Let me get this straight. Gill and Mack both want the book, but we don't know why. And now Q has offered to protect it from some threat that only she knows of, that will occur tonight at midnight?"

"That's the gist of it. And I think with your help, I can discover who the spy is. Let me tell you my plan."

I explained that I had several books in my bag that were similar enough to Ian's that I suspected the others wouldn't be able to tell the difference. I planned to leave one on the table in my room as a decoy while handing another to Q in plain sight of everyone. Meanwhile, I planned to keep the real book in my bag and my bag with me the whole time.

"It's a good plan, but what made you decide to trust me?"

"I've always trusted you, Ky; I just had to keep this to myself because it wasn't my secret to tell. The book is technically Ian's...in a way, it is Ian. So I couldn't just tell you until he accepted that you are on our side. And he has decided that you are. It's not my fault it took him longer to come to that conclusion than it did for me."

Kyro wrapped his arms around me and gently kissed my forehead. He then rested his forehead on mine, sighing. "I don't think you understand what I'm feeling. It's so hard to explain."

"I'm willing to listen if you want to try." After months of avoiding this conversation with Race, I found that I anticipated having it with Kyro.

"Just being around you brings out feelings in me that I thought were dead. Being near you, holding you, kissing you. I'm afraid of what will happen once this quest is over." He looked sad, forlorn even, with that last statement.

"What do you mean? What do you think will happen?"

"I'm afraid that I'm falling in love with you and that I'll lose you when this quest ends."

"Did you just say...wait...say that again?" My eyes got big, and my mouth dropped open in surprise.

"I'm afraid you'll leave me when the quest is complete."

"Not that part, the other part."

"I'm falling in love with you, Zoey."

"Oh, Kyro," I sighed as I threw my arms around his neck and kissed him hard on the mouth. "I've been fighting with myself over whether I should tell you or not, but I think I'm falling for you, too."

He brought his lips to mine again, this time slowly, gently, almost a painful teasing. When we parted, he said, "Then let's trap us a spy so that we can move onto more important things."

Gill

I KNEW IT WAS a risky move to try and steal the book tonight, but I had no choice. I had received a message that my love had been taken. I knew that this was my punishment for failure.

I couldn't let anything happen to my darling. I had to get the book tonight, no matter what it took. The message had promised that I would be reunited with my love if I only brought the book to its rightful owner. We both knew that wasn't true—the angry ogre I worked for didn't have an ownership stake in the book. I knew it, and he knew it. But it didn't matter. He had ensured my cooperation by taking the one person I couldn't live without.

I overheard Q talking to Zoey about the book. To be fair, I only overheard it because I bugged Zoey's room to get more information about where she hid the book. Anyway, I knew that I had done a pretty good job of throwing Q off my trail if she was suspicious but couldn't say who she suspected. Successful or not, by the end of the night, they would all know how I had betrayed their trust. It did no good to beat myself up about it. I had been forced into this and had no choice but to finish it.

I waited in my room, in my bed with the covers drawn, pretending to be sleeping. I needed the others to be asleep before I broke into Zoey's room. I worked on the duplicity spell and decided I'd use it tonight to appear as though I was still in my bed when all this went down. As long as no one saw me, it could work. I had tested the duplicity spell out a few days ago up on the deck. It had worked perfectly. I had been able to keep it up just long enough to make my way to Kyro's library and dig through his books. I couldn't find the invisibility spell I was looking for, though I was convinced Kyro had one. That made my job a little more complex, but at least I knew the duplicity spell would work.

Once I heard Mack's soft snores from his bed, I knew it was nearly time to spring into action. I quietly climbed out of my bed, crept across the floor, and carefully opened the door. I checked the hallway, and there was no one. I made my way down the hall to Zoey's room, pausing outside Q's door. I didn't hear anything, which meant either she was sleeping or she wasn't there. I decided to take my chances and move on to searching Zoey's room. I had a sleep spell prepared to ensure I wasn't caught in the act.

I opened the door to her room, and it was empty. I guessed the attraction between her and Kyro might have been more powerful than I initially thought. I would search the room, and once I was sure the book wasn't there, I would move to the next room until I found it. I trashed the room, hunting for the book. I overturned the bookshelves, the bed, the dresser, the table but found nothing.

Once I was convinced it was not anywhere in this room, I opted to check Q's room next. It had looked like someone else had already gone through Zoey's things before I arrived, so it was the logical choice. I eased back into the hallway again, keeping an eye out for anyone coming out of the rooms. I silently crept down to Q's door, opened it quickly, and slipped inside. It appeared that no one was here either. Where could she be? I didn't wait long for the answer, as she came out of the bathroom just a moment later.

She looked startled to see me but not surprised. "I knew you'd come looking for the book. I've been onto you since the jungle. You'll never find it—I've hidden it somewhere safe."

I snarled at her in response. "You think you can stop me? I will have that book. You will give it to me, or I'll take it from you." And with that, I lunged at her. She punched me in the jaw, knocking me back against the wall. I recovered quickly and swung back at her. I wasn't very good at hand-to-hand combat, so I misjudged the distance and swung wide. She took advantage of that and landed a kick to my kidneys.

I tried to back her into a corner to gain an advantage, but she just kept moving. Every time I thought I had landed a punch, she blocked it. I was getting worn out quickly, but I could tell she was starting to lose steam as well. I caught her off guard with a leg sweep and then clocked her in the face as she fell. She was only down for a minute, rolling over and then popping back up.

She came at me hard then, fists flying. I tried to block them, but she was physically stronger than me. I heard the crack as her blow landed on my nose. The pain was excruciating. I saw stars for a minute, and that was all it took for her to pin me on the floor. She relaxed a bit once she had me pinned and wiped her hand across her lip where I had managed to bust it. I made myself lie perfectly still while she stared down at me. I waited until she shifted her weight to get comfortable, and then I bucked like a wild horse and threw her off me.

I knew she had me bested in a physical match; she had more than proven that. But I still had magic. I kept her attention focused on me and levitated a chair behind her. At the exact moment, I slammed the chair into the back of her head, and I threw the sleep spell at her. I knew if one failed, the other would work. I didn't expect both to work so well. She started to cry out from the chair's impact but was knocked unconscious by the spell before she had the chance to make the sound entirely. Her body slumped to the floor before I could catch her. If she woke up, she'd be in a lot of pain tomorrow. I wasn't entirely sure that she would survive that blast, though. I'd hit her harder than I had intended.

I started tearing the room apart, looking for the book. It wasn't here. How could it not be here? I'd heard them arrange for Zoey to give it to Q at midnight. There had to be somewhere else I hadn't thought to look. I slowly walked every inch of the room, looking for false panels or other places to hide it. I found a small cubby that I had missed the first time through. It was hidden behind a false door next to the bed. Sure enough, the book was tucked safely inside.

I took one last look around the room before I left. The pool of blood that was forming under Q's head was not a good sign. I hoped that someone woke after I left and found her, so she didn't die. I couldn't chance to heal her, though. The boss's men would be waiting on me as it was. I'd already taken too long.

I walked out on the deck and stopped to look around. They should be here by now. I knew I was running late and hoped they hadn't left without me. I walked the length of the boat silently, checking for the lifeboat that would take me to my destiny. As soon as I spotted it, I knew something was wrong. There was no way the boss would have let Shannon come to get me, but there she was. "Get in." She wasn't going to mince words.

I climbed into the boat. "Why are you here? It was just supposed to be these guys."

She looked at me impatiently and turned around. "You didn't hurt him, did you?" She asked quietly.

She didn't turn to look at me as I answered. "Nowhere near as bad as you did." She nodded without turning around, and the goons started rowing the lifeboat away from Kyro's boat.

Zoey

KYRO AND I DECIDED that it would be best to stay together as much as possible after everything happened, both because we wanted to and to protect the book. Kyro invited me to share his room with him because his bed was larger, and we would have more privacy. I didn't have anything but my bag, so it was an easy move for me to make. I had been carrying my bag around with me since my visit from Q. It didn't take us long to choose two of my blank journals to use as the decoy books and set a trap for the spy. Once we caught him or her, we would find out who they were working for and what they wanted with the book.

When everything was set up, the first blank journal was placed on the table in my room, with some papers and books of Kyro's somewhat hiding it. Now I just had to wait for Q to stop by and pick up the second. Then Kyro and I would use a scrying spell to track both books and see who the spy turned out to be. I didn't like being away from Kyro or the book, but it was needed to make this believable. I entrusted my bag to him while I waited in my room for Q.

There was a light tap on the door. I knew it was Q. "Hurry, come in." I opened the door just enough for her to come inside, closing it quickly behind her. Then I made sure I positioned myself in a way that blocked her view of the bed we had made up to look as though I was sleeping in it.

"I wasn't sure if you'd still want to go through with this or not." Q had expected me to decide this was a bad idea. "I'll take care of the book until morning, and then once everyone is up for the day, I'll bring it back."

"Thank you. I don't know how I would be able to keep the book safe without your help." I had to be convincing if this was going to work. Although I hoped the spy wasn't Q. I liked her and wanted to trust her. I handed her the second decoy book, and she quietly left the room. I waited a little longer than initially planned just to make sure she made it back to her room, and then I carefully opened the door just enough to see if the hallway was clear. It was, so I quickly crept across the hall and into Kyro's room. Since we had fixed the bed, it would appear that I was sleeping if someone came in looking for the book.

I wasn't sure how long we would have to wait before anything happened or if our plan would even work. Kyro and I didn't want to make any noise while waiting, so we communicated by notes.

Me: *Do you think this is going to work?*

Him: *I guess we'll find out soon enough.*

Me: *Who do you think is the spy?*

Him: *I'm not sure. It could be any of the three of them.*

Me: *I understand. Did you hear that?*

Kyro put his finger to his lips, indicating that he had heard the soft click of my door across the hall. He was getting ready to start the scrying spell when a soft knock came at his door.

The brogue gave away who was at the door as he spoke. "Ky, are you awake? I think something is wrong. Zoey isn't in her room, and I can't find Gill."

Kyro opened the door, revealing Mack standing on the other side of it. "Come in. But be silent, and I'll explain." Mack entered the room, looking both surprised and relieved when he saw me.

"Oh, love, I'm glad you're safe. I thought the worst when I saw how your room had been torn apart." Mack grabbed me into a bear hug, and for a moment, I thought he was about to cry.

Kyro and I looked at each other over Mack's head. I guess the plan had worked. "Did you notice the books on the table? Had any of them been disturbed?" I pulled back from Mack's embrace and looked at him. I had to know if the bait had been taken.

"There were no books on the table or anywhere else in the room. The bed had been tossed, and papers were all over. It looked as though someone was searching for something."

"Good," Kyro responded and then began to set up the scrying spell. As he worked, I filled Mack in on what was happening. Kyro located the decoy book I had given to Q first. It appeared to be in her room. "Well, there's one book found. Should we verify its location or find the other first?"

"Let's find the other, and then we can go deal with this one at a time." I was trying to think logically but was relieved that it looked as though Q was in the clear.

Kyro nodded and continued the spell. "I can't find the other book. It must not be on board the boat anymore. But we aren't docked, so I'm not sure how it would have left the boat. Unless someone helped it and had help from someone else." I think Mack and I both knew what he was thinking, but neither of us said anything.

"Let's go check on the one you found, and we'll have our answer." Mack was the voice of reason. So we carefully left Kyro's room, creeping down the hall to Q's room. I had brought my backpack with the actual book in it for safekeeping.

"Let me." I figured if I knocked and asked for the book while the guys hid on either side of the door, we would know what had happened. I knocked gently and waited a moment for Q to answer. There was no response from inside the room. I looked at Kyro and Mack, raising my eyebrows as if to ask, "What next?" They both nodded, and I tried the door. It opened, and we went inside to look around.

The room had been tossed, just like mine. We found Q lying knocked out on the floor beside the bed, with her hands and feet tied and a gag in her mouth. I ran to her and made sure she was breathing. After Mack performed a quick healing spell, she was alive and would recover, but she was out cold. We searched the room carefully, looking for the decoy book I had given her. Finally, Kyro pulled out the scrying spell, and we were able to locate it. I don't think we could have found it without that spell, though. Q had kept true to her word and hidden the book very well to protect it. A wave of relief washed over me with the knowledge that I could trust her. It appeared that we had our answer; Gill must be the spy. If we could catch him before he got away, maybe we could get some answers. We spent a few minutes setting Q's room to rights and then untying her and putting her into bed. Mack did a rudimentary healing spell and said she would likely wake with a headache in the morning but would be fine after a night's sleep.

Once Q was settled, I set up a perimeter spell to alert us if either she got up or someone else came in the room while we were gone. We had each been working with Kyro on learning some simple spells that we could do for protection while we learned to fight from Q and Mack. With the magic in place and checked by Kyro, we headed up the stairs to the deck. The moon was covered mainly by the clouds, making it darker than it had been the past few nights. We looked around for Gill, but he was nowhere to be found. After we checked all around the boat, Kyro called to his mermaid friends. The male I had seen with him the night I found out about his ability to change from human to merman came to the surface to see what Kyro needed.

"Mateo, did you see anyone leave the boat tonight?" Kyro asked him as he leaned over the railing.

Mateo looked around as he spoke. "I saw one of your crew get on a passing rowboat a while ago. I think they headed that way." He pointed north, the opposite direction we had been heading. "Why did he leave with those guys? They were super creepy. And he looked nervous, like he expected to be followed, or as if he didn't want to go with them."

"Did you see if he was carrying anything with him?" I couldn't help but ask. I needed to know if he had taken the bait or not. Especially with the extra something Ian had helped me add to the decoy book.

Mateo looked at me carefully. "He did have a leather-bound journal with him. I wouldn't have noticed, but the guys in the rowboat kept trying to get it from him, and he kept telling them he would only give it to the Chairman. It seemed odd."

"Good. At least now we know for sure that Gill was the spy and that he was working for the Order." It was a relief to know that the plan had worked.

"We're not sure why he's working for the Order, but we also aren't going to worry about that right now. He's long gone, and we have a quest to complete. It will take a few hours, at least for them to realize he took the wrong book. Let's use that to our advantage and move on to the next phase." Kyro was definitely in charge, and he made good points.

"Um, Ky, we may have more time than you think." I figured now was a good time to let him know about Ian's backup plan. "Ian decided to enchant the decoy, so they won't know right away that it's not the real book. He said it's a simple spell that will show a map and some clues when they open it, but the clues will just lead the Order around in circles for a while. It'll be hard for them to tell it's not the real book. That should buy us some time. I'm sorry I didn't tell you before. I thought we'd be able to catch him in the act, and that wouldn't be needed. But I'm glad now that Ian insisted."

"That's great news, Zoey. Now we have time to plan our next phase out and move forward. We should get some rest now so we can move first thing in the morning. I'll take the first watch."

"No, Ky, I'll take the first watch. You and Zoey need to rest. The majority of the spell work will fall to you, and she has to be ready for whatever comes at us. I can do with less sleep, so I'll take watch." It was hard to argue with Mack, especially when he made it easier for me to spend time with Kyro. Kyro agreed because after he spoke with Mateo briefly, we headed downstairs to his room.

"What did you say to Mateo?" I asked hesitantly.

Kyro grinned at me. "I asked him to help Mack keep an eye on things up there. He told me he was planning on hanging around no matter who took the watch."

"Good. I'm glad Mack isn't alone up there." The door closed behind me, and suddenly I was wrapped up in Kyro's arms once again. It was becoming my favorite place to be.

He pressed his lips to mine gently. "I'm so glad you were in here with me instead of over there when Gill took the book. I can't imagine what I would have done if he had taken you." He kissed me again, this time deepening the kiss and running his hands up into my hair. "I know this isn't the time for us to be together, but I don't know how much more I can stand. It makes me crazy risking you the way we did tonight. I'm just glad you weren't in your room."

"I completely agree. I want to be with you. And we will. But we have to get some rest now so we can find the right island tomorrow. With any luck, we can get through whatever puzzles are there and get back here with no problems." I knew it wouldn't be that easy, but I was hopeful.

Jack

CALLIOPE HAD THOUSANDS OF people living on her and even more visiting daily. There was no way the rumor mill should have picked this up as quickly as it had. I sighed my frustration as I overheard yet another conversation about Zoey being hunted for Race's murder. It was all I could do to refrain from snatching up these people and ripping their heads off their shoulders for the things they were saying about her. I headed down to my office, barely keeping myself in check. My plan for the day had been to take it easy, but if these rumors were even remotely true, that would change everything.

With reports of the Planet Patrol closing in on Zoey's location, I knew I was running out of time. My hands shook with anticipation, and a small trickle of sweat danced down my spine. They were claiming that she was armed and dangerous and were discussing a possible shoot-to-kill plan. I couldn't let that happen. I had to get that machine running now. There was no time to waste.

The door to my office opened slowly...too slowly. Between that and the walk down here, I'd had too much time to think. If I couldn't pull this off, Zoey would be behind bars. Once I was finally inside, I locked the door and disabled the override. I couldn't be disturbed. I was so crazed with the thoughts that were running rampant in my head that I almost forgot to disable the cameras. That was bad. But I caught it before moving the bookcase and revealing the secret passage that led to the catacombs. Race and I had been the only ones who knew about it. Right after his death, I had set some traps just if he had let his boss know about our private area, but every time I went down there, the safeguards were still in place.

When I learned of Zoey being accused of murder, I threw caution mainly to the wind and began using the secret space for a project designed to help her. I had been stashing food stores in one room for a while and began to bring other items down as well. At this point, it was so well stocked, I could have lived there for decades. But it wasn't for me, and I hoped it wouldn't take decades to clear her name.

I'd been working on this gadget in secret for weeks now. It was almost done. I just had to work out the connections in the transponder. Yeah, it would be a lot easier just to order one. And faster, too, with Amazon's new galactic shipping. But it was riskier as well. So far, no one seemed to suspect what I was up to when I locked myself in my office these days. They just figured I was taking Race's death and Zoey's disappearance hard. In reality, I'd been smuggling pieces down here to build a transporter. Being forced to craft each component in the musty basement of the space station was rough. Not being able to use the good tools that would make it go faster was irritating.

I had to remind myself that whining never got me anywhere. I needed to find the courage and get this done. Zoey may not know it, but her life was depending on me finishing this thing. I worked until I hit a wall. My eyes were crossed and droopy, and concentration was a long-lost memory. *I'll close my eyes for a minute and then get back to it, I thought to myself.*

I woke hours later, face down on my workbench, with a soldering iron in my hand. Luckily I hadn't managed to turn it on before sleep took me, or I may have awoken to a much different scene.

To keep up appearances, I made my way back to my office to see if I had messages to deal with. Once my minor work issues were taken care of, I arranged to take the rest of the day off and, after securing my office, returned to my room. A short nap and a shower were just what the doctor ordered. With those tasks out of the way, I secured my room, disabled the camera that Race shouldn't have installed in the first place, and opened the closet door. It was a tight fit, but I walked through, pushing on the plate in the back wall that would allow me access to the hidden tunnel system leading to my workspace.

I followed the tunnels until I was behind the museum vault. I hoped I had timed this correctly, or I was about to get myself busted. I hit the portable jammer to disengage the security cameras and alarms. I slipped through the passage hidden behind a row of bookcases in the back of the vault. I could only use the jammer for two minutes at a time without risking security noticing the monitors were blank. I had to work fast. I needed three books—one on engineering, one on healing, and one on the effects of gamma radiation. I needed to be prepared for anything.

I stayed hunched over while I looked for the books. It helped that I had hacked the catalog and knew approximately where each book should be. In a minute and a half, I had two of the three books in my possession. The gamma radiation book wasn't where it should have been. *There's no time to waste hunting for it. I have to get out of here before the jammer cuts out.* With that thought, I ran for the secret panel. Just as it clicked closed behind me, I heard the vault door open. "Hello? Is someone there? No one is allowed inside the vault without an escort. Hello? Hmm, I guess I heard things." I heard the vault door close again and breathed a sigh of relief.

At least it wasn't a total loss. I got two of the books I need. I'll just have to go back later for the third one. I headed back to my workshop to do some research and planning. *But what happened to the third book?* I couldn't get that thought out of my head. I couldn't imagine someone else needing a book on gamma radiation at the same time that I did. Of course, I was probably just being paranoid. Given the situation, who could blame me?

I sat down at my workbench and opened the engineering book. *Let's see, where's that section on transponders? Ah, here it is.* I laid the open book on top of one of the dozen that were already piled up on the bench in front of me. Then I opened the book on healing. After scanning the table of contents, I realized this might just be the one I had been looking for. It had recipes for tonics that would help with fatigue from transportation. I bookmarked that page and set the book aside in favor of the engineering book. I read the section on transponders and then hunted up the diagrams in the appendix to see what the section was talking about.

During my research, I realized I needed that missing book more than I thought. The gamma radiation calculations just weren't making sense. I needed the details in that book to figure out the math of it all. I began to organize another secret raid on the library when I came across a different text outlining a transporter that combines science and magic. According to what I read there, I wouldn't need the missing book at all. However, I would need a specific amulet, which was an antique. I spent the better part of two hours researching where to find this amulet and precisely what it looked like.

The amulet required for the combination teleporter was about six inches in diameter, with a swirling pattern carved into it. It was made of onyx, typically used for abjuration, and was approximately 600 years old. Upon further research, I learned that the stone's swirling pattern was a Norse pattern carved upon it for protection. The pattern was called a triskele and represented the world, the otherworld, and the celestial world. The magic represented by this symbol would assist the transporter in moving a person across space and possibly time.

I spent a bit of time searching for the exact location of the amulet. When I didn't find anything definitive, I decided to visit the museum and see if I could convince the girl taking care of it to help me. In the best-case scenario, I would find the amulet there and have to steal it. Worst case scenario, I would get some help locating the charm and have to steal it from somewhere else. Either way, I was sure the process wouldn't be easy and would involve theft. Lucky for me, I was trained for just this.

A call to the museum afforded me some much-needed information. The girl taking over for Zoey was Elena, and she was working in the mornings. I made an appointment for a tour in the morning and then decided to rest for the night and prepare questions that wouldn't make it obvious what I was after. I figured I'd also look for the missing book while I was there. It couldn't hurt to be as prepared as possible for using this machine I was building.

I got up early in the morning, showered, and headed to the museum. I knew from the time I spent doing surveillance on the area that Elena tended to show up early. I wanted to catch her off guard and see if I could find the amulet. I had made the appointment under the guise of looking for that book on gamma radiation. I knew I could flirt with her if needed and get her to show me around the whole place. Before Zoey left, Elena was her apprentice and apparently may have had a crush on me. I wasn't above using that to my advantage.

I arrived just as Elena was unlocking the doors. "Good morning. Am I early?" I winked at her as I spoke, and her cheeks pinked.

"Oh, Jack, um…you are a little early, but it's fine. Let me just get logged in and the lights on. You can come inside and take a look around if you want to while you wait." This was going to be easier than I thought. If I could find the amulet on my own and palm it, then I could just get the short tour and head back to work. I followed her inside and began to wander around while she went into the office.

I glanced at my comm device to see the picture of the amulet. I had to remember what it looked like so I could hunt for it. I started in the Norse section, and after a few minutes, I had located what I was sure was the amulet. Unfortunately, it was in a locked glass case. I knew from experience that those cases were also employing a pressure-sensitive plate under the objects that would set off an alarm if they were removed. I would need a better plan. There was no way I could just do a quick snatch and run without getting caught.

I was pondering this as Elena walked up behind me. "You find something you like?" She joked.

"Well, yeah, I did—" I stated bluntly as I looked her up and down. It had been too long since I'd been with a woman. I needed to be careful with my flirting. Her cheeks turned pink again, and she stammered a bit. I took advantage of the moment and pulled her to me clumsily for a kiss. As I pressed my lips to hers and teased them apart to allow my tongue to dance with hers, I backed her into the display case. I regretted what I had to do, but I knew going into this that my relationships would always take a back seat to Zoey's safety. I managed just enough passion in the kiss to warrant using Elena to knock the display over and bust the glass. She didn't break the kiss immediately, and I couldn't help but groan in response.

She met my passion with her own, and before I knew what I was doing, I had her pinned up against the wall next to the mess of broken glass and artifacts. My left hand was kneading her breast as my right hand searched for the hem of her skirt. I thought my erection might kill me if it wasn't taken care of quickly. Just as I got my hand under her dress and found the edge of her panties, she broke the kiss and pushed me away. "I'm sorry, I shouldn't have done that. I'm not usually like that. Please forgive me. I'll just go." I was mortified that I had almost lost control and forced myself on her because of one kiss.

"Don't go. I just didn't want you to get cut with all this glass. Give me a minute to see to cleaning up this mess, and we can pick this up in the office where we won't be disturbed. Unless you don't want to?" I stared at her in disbelief, and it was my turn to be speechless.

"I, uh, no, that's fine, I'll wait." She sashayed away to get the cleaning bot, making sure to wiggle her apple-shaped ass in just the right way to make sure I didn't go anywhere. As soon as she was out of visual range, I hit the jammer and picked up the amulet. I had the charm in my jacket pocket when she came back with the bot. She set it to clean up the mess, took my hand, and led me into the office, locking the door behind us.

She pushed me down onto the couch, removing her shoes before climbing on my lap. I leaned forward and took off my jacket, carefully laying it to the side out of the way. I couldn't have the mood ruined by her finding the amulet in my pocket. I already knew I would feel like an ass after this was all said and done...it didn't need to be any worse. With my jacket off, she pushed me against the back of the couch, grinding against my erection. I groaned in response, and she leaned toward me, taking my lips in an intense kiss.

This time her tongue was the one in charge, coaxing my lips open so our tongues could tango. Her hands went from the sides of my face, into my hair, and then down my chest and torso. It seemed as though she couldn't get enough of touching me. I felt the need to return the favor, so I let my hands have free reign with her body as well. I fisted one hand in her hair as the other kneaded her breast. She groaned into my mouth in pleasure and ground herself into me more. I moaned back and removed my hand from her hair. I sent it traveling down her, stopping to knead her other breast and then slipping it around to cup her round ass. I pulled her more forcefully into my erection.

I slid my hand under her skirt, tugged her panties to the side, and began to stroke her moist center. She began to moan and rubbed up and down on my hand until I pulled it away. I unbuttoned her shirt, slipped it off her, and started to trail kisses down her neck. By the time I got to her full breasts, I had removed her bra as well. She tugged at my shirt, anxious to get it off me. I obliged and then turned my attention back to her taut nipples. As I suckled on one, I teased the other with pinches and strokes. Then I switched sides. Once I had her to a point where she was putty in my hands, I flipped her over on the couch, sliding between her legs. I removed her skirt, and she arched up for me to take her panties next. When I had all of her remaining clothes off, I kissed her again as her hands fumbled with my belt and pants. She seemed desperate to get me naked, and I wasn't going to stop her.

I continued to kiss her while I helped her remove my pants and boxers. Then I began to trail tiny bites down her chest and stomach, following the heat down to her center. I teased her with my tongue and fingers until she cried out in pleasure and was begging me to enter. I thrust into her moistness, feeling the muscles contract as I stretched her to her limits. Still, inside her, I righted us to a sitting position on the couch, where she could ride me to her satisfaction. That was precisely what she did, and I managed to finish just after she did. For a minute, I wasn't sure I'd be able to hold out, but then I considered the fact that I was deceiving her, and that helped.

After my encounter with Elena in the office, it was a relief to head back to my room and shower. She had managed to locate the missing book the day before, so the entire trip was a success. I planned to spend my evening reading about fighting the effects of gamma radiation and studying the amulet as well as the text that detailed it. I still felt like an ass, so I sent Elena a message asking if she'd like to go to dinner with me. I knew it would be hard to keep the truth from her if we got involved, but I didn't want it to seem like I was just after some random fling.

Before I could get a response, my comm device went off. It was a secure call from Mama Bear. "Yes, ma'am, what can I do for ya?" There was an amused chuckle from the other end of the line.

"Jack, please tell me you have a plan. They are closing in on her, and I'm fearful of what will happen to her if they get there first. I can't intervene."

Well, this wasn't ideal, but I knew things would go from bad to worse before we were done. "The plan is almost in place. I just have a few kinks to work out, and I'll have her secured."

I broke the connection and got back to work. I had to get the gamma radiation issue taken care of and figure out exactly where and how the amulet fit into the equation.

I slid the flux capacitor into place. The soft click told me when it was fully seated. It was now or never. I stepped back away from the platform to the workbench where the remote control sat. My hand closed around the small metal box. I turned the dials to ensure I had locked onto Zoey. If this worked, she would be here with me in less than a minute. With a deep inhale of breath, I pressed the button.

There was a blinding flash of light. An invisible wave of force knocked me back into the wall, then slid down on my ass. That hurt. *What the hell just happened.* I shook my head to clear it from the explosion. *No, not an explosion...Zoey!* I jumped to my feet and ran to the platform. She was lying across it on the floor. There was no movement; it was impossible to tell if she was breathing or not.

I sank to my knees, my hand instantly searching for a pulse. It was light and thready, but it was there. She was alive. Barely, but more importantly, she was safe. I scooped her into my arms and carried her to the bedroom I'd made for her down here. She couldn't exactly go back to her rooms upstairs, where anyone could see her. I laid her down gently on the bed, left the note I had written for her if she woke while I was gone, and left the room. I locked the door behind me. I was confident I'd catch hell for that as well, but I couldn't have her running off half-cocked. I needed to explain everything.

With her safely on Calliope, I had more time to figure out the rest of the plan. I knew I couldn't keep her hidden away forever, but I wasn't sure yet how I would clear her name. I needed more time. That's precisely what this was about; I had just bought us some time. I followed the tunnels to Zoey's room, hit the button on the jammer, and went inside through the closet. I gathered her clothing and toiletries before slipping the panel back in place and heading back to my room.

It was early, and I needed to report to work this morning. Since I was on camera entering my room, I figured I should be on camera leaving. I gathered what I would need for the next few days, placed it in a duffel bag, and sat the pack in the hidden tunnel. I would come back for my stuff and Zoey's after my shift. Now I had to arrange for some vacation time and convince everyone that I've left Calliope for a couple of weeks. That should be enough time to figure out how to fix this mess, especially if I pull my actual boss into the mix. I was sure that wouldn't be pleasant either, but I couldn't see a way around it. I'd make that call later, though.

After arranging for three weeks of vacation, explaining that I would travel, and try to get things figured out since I still wasn't over Race's death, I headed back to my room. I had purchased a shuttle ticket and was supposed to leave at midnight. That gave me an alibi to stay in my room today, as I would need to sleep to be up that late. I would have to make it look like I got on the shuttle and then sneak back into the tunnels. Since Race and I had done it when we were teens, I knew it was possible.

With the plan in place, I felt calmer than I had in weeks. I still hadn't gotten to the bottom of Stephen's death, and that bothered me. He was just a security guard. There was no reason to kill him. I only couldn't find the proof I needed to make a move—yet. But I would. I took the usual protocols after shutting my door. My hands were sweaty as I dialed the number on the secure communicator.

As usual, two rings, and it was answered. "Yes?" Once again, the voice sounded irritable, as though I had interrupted something.

"I got her before they did." I waited for the response.

"How did you manage to get there before they did? They were on their way to the last known location two hours ago."

Now it was my turn to chuckle. "I have my ways. And before you ask, I'm not giving up her location. They can't have her, and neither can you. Not until I've cleared her name. Which brings me to the reason for my call."

An exasperated sigh told me I might get what I wanted. "Are you going to tell me your plan or make me guess?"

"I'm not telling you all of it. What I need from you is more intel on the Order. I need proof that the Chairman was here the day Race was killed." Silence met my question. "So you have the proof already. I figured as much. And you'd let the Patrol take her in for his crime? I expected more from you."

More silence, then I heard a throat clear. "You know that's not fair. I can't protect Zoey forever. That's what I have you for. As for the proof you're requesting, I don't have it. I know it was him, but proving it has become a challenge."

I didn't believe her, but there was nothing I could do to make her share the information I was asking for either. I would have to play along with the cat and mouse thing a bit longer. "I understand. Can you at least see what you can come up with?

I've been searching through security feeds and have nothing to go on. Well, except for the two dead bodies."

There was a cough, and it sounded as though she was choking. "Did you say two bodies? Why do I only know about Race then? Who is the other one? What happened? Tell me everything."

"Ugh, I knew this would come up at some point. I was hoping to have more evidence before we discussed it, though. The other dead body belongs to one of the security guards. His name was Stephen, and he was investigating Race's death. I found a lead, and before I could get to him and warn him to watch his back, someone else got him. He was tortured and killed."

"That's not good. Are there more operatives on Calliope? Where did you find a lead?" There was the impatient tone I was used to.

"There may be operatives here. Or the Chairman sent goons to take care of Stephen before he could expose the Order. I'm not sure yet. I'll share my intel once the heat is off. I don't even trust a secure connection for data transfer. Maybe I'm paranoid, but maybe I'm not."

With a promise of any assistance possible, she ended the call. I showered before taking my bags and heading back to the tunnels.

Zoey

I woke up in a strange bed, in an unfamiliar room. My head hurt, and I wasn't sure what had happened, but I had a nagging feeling I forgot something. Something important. I had no idea what time it was or even what day it was. *How long was I asleep?* I sat up and took a look around the stark room. There was no furniture except for the bed and a small table with paper on it. *Maybe that's a place to start,* I thought to myself as I walked over to the table and picked up the page. It was a note from Jack. Something seemed strange about that, but I couldn't quite place it. I unfolded the letter and read it.

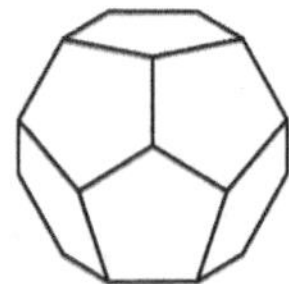

Zoey,

I know you won't understand what happened, but I brought you here to protect you. The Patrol was closing in, and I had to get you out of there, so we have time to clear your name. Please just stay calm. I'll be back as soon as I can. There's a snack here to tide you over.

—Jack

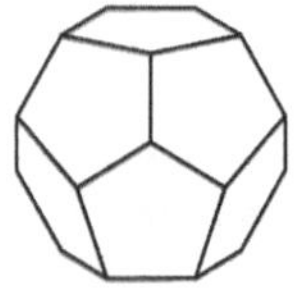

I had no idea what he was talking about. And what did he mean? I need to stay calm? I had to find him and ask. I set the note down and walked across the room to the door. I turned the handle, and nothing happened. Jack had locked me in here. There was something strange going on here. Why would the Patrol be after me? Had I done something that I couldn't remember? There were so many questions, and I had absolutely no answers. All I could do was wait for Jack and hope he could explain what was happening.

I sat back down on the bed and picked up a notebook and pencil from the nightstand. I felt like I forgot something important. Mama had always told me that if I ever felt that way, I should just free write until it came to me. So that's what I planned to do. I had to figure out what I was forgetting and why Jack had locked me in this room. After writing everything in my head, spending two hours going over absolutely everything I could think of, I was tapped. I had no idea what was going on. I had nothing else to do, so I ended up falling asleep and having the strangest dream.

I was on a boat with a tall, crimson-haired woman, a short, flame-haired man with braids down his back, and the most gorgeous man I'd ever seen. He was tall, with dark curls and olive skin. They all seemed to know me, though I couldn't place how. I had never even seen a boat in person before. I hadn't even been off Calliope since I arrived when I was a child. But it was a dream, so I guessed that didn't matter.

We were searching for something. It was important. And there was a book. It looked like we were talking to the book. The whole thing was so bizarre. I wondered why Race or Jack wasn't in this dream with me. My best guess was that I had been feeling stifled here lately and wanted to escape. I decided to see where this dream took me. After all, it's just a dream, right? Dreams can't hurt you.

So I followed along with what was happening until the scene changed. I was in a dungeon with a wicked sense of déjà vu. I was sure I had been here before. But again, that wasn't possible. I just had this nagging feeling that I was in danger, but I couldn't place why. There were people chained to the walls, and they had all been tortured to varying degrees. The air was cold and damp, causing me to shiver. It seemed strange that the temperature in a dream could cause a shiver, but maybe it was just a creepy scene.

I wandered the room, taking stock of everything I saw. Then I heard it...a voice that I was sure I had heard before—yet I had no clue to whom it belonged. It was raspy and harsh, "I see you've come back to me, my child."

As lost and confused as I was, I wasn't sure that playing along with this dream would be a good thing. "I'm not sure who you are. Can you explain to me how I got here?"

A dark chuckle filled the air. "You can play dumb if you want, child, but I have you now. Your friends won't be able to save you this time. As for the how of it, I thought you had figured that out the last time we spoke."

I turned circles looking for the source of the voice. "What do you mean, my friends won't be able to save me this time? Have I been here before? What do you want from me?" I knew it was probably pointless to ask, but I wasn't sure what else to do since this disembodied voice seemed to think it owned me now.

"You aren't playing dumb, are you? Somehow you've lost your memories. Interesting. Then allow me to explain, child. Have a seat."

Suddenly the room changed. I was sitting on a fluffy white velvet couch in a cozy, sun-filled sitting room. "Oh, this is lovely. So much better than that disgusting dungeon." I ran my hands over the velvet, enjoying the feel of it against my skin. This was the strangest dream I'd ever had.

The voice suddenly appeared as a cloud of smoke and vapor. It was a slowly swirling mass of blue and gray. Its motions were elegant and comforting. I wasn't sure how I knew it was the voice, but somehow I was sure of it. I still had an uneasy feeling about this voice, but I was no longer on edge the way I was in the dungeon.

"Child, let me tell you about what you've been involved in. Then you'll realize I'm only trying to help you." I settled in on the sofa and listened intently to the now smooth voice. "You were helping me to look for a lost artifact, a book that had been misplaced by my family many centuries ago. Once you found it, a wizard put a spell on you and convinced you that I would use the book's power for evil purposes. He turned you against me, and you were taking the book to him. Where did you put the book, child?"

I didn't remember anything about a book. The only remotely interesting thing that had happened recently was the new shipment of artifacts from Earth that had arrived on Calliope a few days ago. I hadn't yet begun the process of cataloging and inventorying them, though, so I had no idea what was there. I decided to try to bluff my way out of this. "The book is safe. I can't tell you where because anyone could be listening to us right now." I hoped the voice would buy my little white lie and go on with the story.

"No matter, we can deal with retrieval of the book later. It's enough for me to know I have you back." The swirls of blue and grey seemed calmer once I said the book was safe.

"Is this why the Planet Patrol has been after me?" I wondered out loud.

"The Patrol is chasing you? Oh, child, I wish you had come to me sooner. What happened?" Great, he didn't know either. I figured I was on my own for that part. And possibly the rest as well, since I wasn't sure how I felt about what the voice had just told me.

"I'm not sure. I woke up today with no recent memories. I don't even know for sure what day it is. I just have a feeling I've lost

some time. Especially with what you've just told me about the book and the wizard. I have no memories of the wizard at all." I left out that I had no memories of the book either, but I was trying to get info out of this guy and didn't think he'd be too willing to talk if he thought I had nothing to offer him.

"But you're certain the book is safe? It hasn't fallen into the wrong hands?"

I nodded. "I'm certain it's safe."

"Good, then we have work to do. I'll need your help from outside this realm."

I paused for a moment, still running my fingers over the supple velvet of the couch. "What do I need to do? And I'm sorry, I can't recall your name or how I even contacted you. What do I do if I need to talk to you again?" I hoped the barrage of questions didn't deter my companion from sharing more information with me.

"I didn't realize your memory loss applied to me as well. I'm sorry, child. How inconsiderate of me. My code name is Smoke, as it's safer than using real names. You called out to me in your dream, and I came to you. That's how we communicate. As for what I need you to do, that's simple. Get the book, and let me know when you're ready to deliver it. I'm sure you don't have it on you because, as you said, it wouldn't be safe. So once you've retrieved it from its hiding spot, let me know, and I will come to you."

I nodded thoughtfully. "That sounds easy enough."

"Then it's settled. I'll give you a boost to get back since your powers seem to be on the fritz, and then you can get to work. I look forward to seeing you soon, child." And before I could ask about my powers, I was thrust back into my body and awoke sitting up.

"What the hell was that?" I said aloud to myself. I picked up the paper and pencil and began detailing every bit of the dream and the strange encounter. Just as I was finishing up my written account of the experience, I heard footsteps. I was hesitant to move toward the door, but I decided it would be better to meet things head-on because I was a captive here. I hid behind the door, turned off the light to give myself an advantage, and waited to see if it would be opened. My body tensed for a fight as the key turned in the lock.

The door swung open, and a figure entered. "What the hell? Why is it so dark?" I pounced before he could get anything else out. In an instant, I was on his back and had him pinned under me on the floor, though he was near twice my size. I think I was in as much shock as he was; I had no idea how I had just done that, without any training or knowledge of self-defense or fighting.

"Well, it's good to know that you've learned some things while you've been gone, Zo, but could you get off my back?"

It took a moment to realize I was sitting on Jack. "Oh, Jack, I'm sorry! I wasn't sure who you were or what was happening here." I removed myself from his back and even helped him up from the floor.

"I see you've been working out." He eyed my now muscular arms accusingly.

"Honestly, Jack, I have no idea what you're talking about. This day has been so strange. Where's Race? Why isn't he here? Please sit with me, and explain it all." I hoped the look on my face was enough to convince him that I had no clue what had happened.

He pulled me into a bear hug and squeezed protectively. I could have sworn there were tears in his eyes. "I don't under-stand. What aren't you telling me?" I asked as I returned the hug.

Jack loosened his grip without letting me go. "Race is dead, Zo. Someone murdered him. The Patrol thinks that someone is you."

I couldn't have heard that right. "What? No, I just saw him yesterday. Race can't be dead. And why would the Patrol think I killed him? What kind of joke is this?" I could tell from his face that Jack was serious. Race was dead. He had been murdered, and the Patrol thought I had been the one to kill him. *Had I killed Race? Was that why I couldn't remember anything?* Jack just looked at me for a minute. I could tell he was fighting back the tears. "Jack, why can't I remember anything? It's obvious I'm missing a chunk of time here, but I have no idea what any of this is about." His eyes got wide, and he ran out the door.

I wasn't sure if I should stay where I was or follow him. Curiosity won out, and I cautiously left the room, heading in the direction Jack had gone. It was at that moment that I realized where I was. This was the old catacombs of Calliope, the secret maze of tunnels that weren't used anymore. They had been originally added as a safety measure when the space station was built and served as a radiation shelter against atomic bombs and anything else that could attack the space station's residents. At least now I knew where I was. I just had to figure out why. I followed Jack through the maze of tunnels for a few minutes until he stopped abruptly at a workbench. He started tearing through books as though his life depended upon finding something specific. I cautiously walked up behind him. "Can I help you find what you're looking for?" He froze and then slowly turned to face me.

"Zoey, oh yeah, I didn't even shut the door. Crap. OK, just don't run off. I'm looking for how to fix this."

I cocked an eyebrow at him. "How to fix what, exactly?"

He looked up again, confused. "You left here six weeks ago, and Race's body was discovered the next day. There are so many people here who think you killed him, and apparently, the Patrol is taking them seriously. That's why they were hunting you."

"So you just decided to build a transporter and rescue me from them? Why?" I wasn't sure how I felt about everything Jack was telling me. He was hiding something.

"Well, I guess it can't hurt to tell you now, especially since you don't remember anything from the last six weeks." As he spoke, he gestured toward two overstuffed chairs sitting across the room next to an electric fireplace that was currently warming the area. I walked over and sat down, waiting for him to continue. "I work for the Resistance. They are fighting against the Order. I'm what you might consider an undercover agent. You are the only reason I'm still on Calliope. I've been here all this time to protect you. I mean, yeah, I'm the head engineer, but only because it was where they could put me so I could protect you. I was recruited right after our graduation party and went through training when I left for school." He paused for a moment so I could process what he had just told me.

"So you've been working for the Resistance this whole time? I have so many questions." It was unreal the things that crossed my mind.

"I know you have questions, and I'll do my best to answer them. I have more to tell you, though. While I was working for the Resistance, Race was working for the Order. I suspected for a while but didn't get the proof until he was killed. He left the proof for me. I think he knew he was going to meet an unfortunate end and decided it would be a chance to come clean." He closed his eyes against the tears that were forming.

"Wait, Race was working for the Order? That brings up even more questions. What's the Order?"

"Sorry, I forgot for a moment that you lost your memory. The Order of Orpheus is an organization trying to control all the magic in the universe and those who have it. The leader is called the Chairman, and I'm pretty sure that's who killed Race. They're trying to steal the book you found in the library." His face suddenly lit up with fear. "You don't have the book. This is bad. This is so bad. I didn't even consider the book when I transported you. I have no idea who has it and if they are good or bad. The Chairman could get it, and then all of this will have been pointless." He was working himself into a full-blown panic now, which was rare for Jack, as he always remained calm and collected.

"Wait, I had the book? And I took it with me when I left here? Where did I go? How did I do all this by myself?" I needed more information from Jack before he completely lost it.

"You weren't really by yourself. You had the book and could talk to the wizard through it. I'm guessing you met up with other people down on Earth, but I'll have to check with my contacts. If you could remember who you were with or where you had been, it would be a lot easier to track down the book before the Chairman does."

"So how do we find out who I was with?" I pressed Jack for answers that he may not have.

"There are two options. I try my contacts and see what they know or can find—that's one option. The other option involves you tapping into your powers and tracking the book. We can do one, or we can try both. I'm game for whatever you want to do."

My jaw dropped in shock. "What do you mean, I can tap into my powers and track the book? I don't have powers. Why does it feel like everyone keeps telling me that I do?"

It was Jack's turn to be in shock. "Who else told you that you have powers? Has someone else been down here? Who was it? Where did they go?" Full panic mode was back on.

"Calm down, Jack. No one has breached your safe house. It was this strange dream I had that I would almost swear wasn't a dream. There was a guy who was nothing but a cloud of smoke and vapor, and he claimed I had been working for him before the book swayed me to the dark side. He wants me to find the book and let him know so he can pick it up. Of course, he doesn't know that I have no idea where it is. But there's something about him that I'm not quite sure I trust."

Jack's eyes narrowed as I spoke. "You aren't going to give him the book, are you?" He seemed nervous. "I'm not sure what I'm going to do at this point. But I trust you, Jack, so if you say I was working with the wizard, I trust that. Could I have been working with this other guy before I found the book? Is that possible?" Jack shook his head slowly. "It sounds to me like the Chairman or one of his men got to you somehow in your dream. I have no doubt you weren't working with anyone else besides the wizard in the book." My face must have given away my confusion. "The wizard isn't actually in the book—he just uses it to communicate with you from the past. It's a long story, and I didn't even believe it at first myself."

"So what about the other guy? Can you use your contacts to find out about him?" Jack nodded, "I can try. If it is the Chairman, I may not have much luck. Did he give you a name or a way to contact him?"

I shrugged. "The guy told me to call him Smoke and said that he would know when I wanted to get back in touch with him. It was very cloak and dagger. Honestly, pretty creepy stuff. I may not remember anything from the past six weeks, but even the way he started the conversation at first made me think we were adversaries, not companions."

Even though I struggled to believe Jack had this secret life, it didn't bother me as much as I had expected. It was almost as though something had happened to change my feelings for him. I felt the familiar longing that for me had always been associated with Jack, but now it seemed as though it was for someone else. Perhaps the other people in my dream had been accurate as well. That thought had my pulse quickening and my mind racing. Who were they, and were they helping me on my quest? How would I find out?

FORTY-FOUR

Jack

I LEFT ZOEY WONDERING how she could figure out what she had forgotten via the amnesia I caused with my transporter. I felt horrible about it, but nothing I read gave me any indication that it was even a possibility. She had a stack of books to read and nothing but time. I needed to have one more conversation with Mama Bear, and then some decisions were made. I made my way to another deserted area of tunnels and made the call.

"Is everything alright, Jack? I'm not used to you calling so frequently." She sounded worried as she should be.

"I want to tell her everything." Silence met my statement. "I know you want to keep it all secret, but she deserves to know. And at the very least, I'm going to give her the package." More silence. "Say something, would you?"

"You need to give her the package. I'll agree to that. I'm not ready for her to know everything just yet. Please. I just need more time. I'll double your monthly stipend."

I didn't like it when she begged. "I didn't ask for more money. I said she deserves to know. You can't argue against that. If you aren't ready, I won't tell her, but I am giving her the package tonight. I'm not sure it'll do much good without the book, though."

"You don't have the book?" Mama Bear seemed to be getting impatient.

"How was I supposed to get the book and Zoey? It's not like I waltzed down to the boat they were on and said, 'Hey Zo, come on, get your stuff, we're leaving.' I didn't know she wouldn't have it on her." There was an audible sigh from the other end of the line. "I know it's not what you wanted to hear, but we'll find it as soon as we clear her name and can be seen out and about again. She's lost all memory of the last six weeks. I'm not sure what I can do to bring it back."

She cleared her throat before answering. "What did you do?"

"Well, you just told me to get her. You didn't tell me how. So I built a transporter from scratch, and it worked. Except for the memory loss thing." I knew this wasn't going to be pleasant. That's why I wasn't planning to share the how of what I had done.

"Do you have any idea how many laws you've broken?! How am I supposed to stop them from coming after you? Did you even consider for a moment that you might be putting her in more danger? What the hell were you thinking?"

I waited until the tirade was over to consider my response.

"I wasn't concerned with breaking the law. The transactions are all untraceable, so that's not an issue. How does this put her in more danger? I saved her from the Patrol. I'm not the bad guy here. What aren't you telling me, Mama Bear?" I was livid at the accusation that Zoey's welfare wasn't my top priority.

"I fear the Patrol will realize I've been feeding you information for personal gain. If that happens, I'll lose my position and my ability to protect the two of you."

I was sure there was more to it than that, but if this was all she wanted me to know for now, so be it. "We'll lay low until everything blows over. I just have to figure out how to get her memories back to find and collect the book. In the meantime, I'm going to give her the package today. If you prefer to have your involvement kept out of it, that's fine. But I know she's going to have questions about where and how I got it."

Mama Bear let out an audible sigh. "I know she'll have questions. You'll have to do your best to answer them without bringing me into it. I'll be in touch again when it's safe. I have to go." The line went dead. That was the closest thing I'd gotten to a "goodbye" in years. I think this was all starting to get to her.

With any luck, we'd be able to find a way to restore Zoey's memories and recover the book before the Patrol realized they had a chance to find it. I made my way back through the tunnels to my room. I hit the jammer and then entered through the secret panel in the back of the closet. I had to retrieve the package so I could give it to Zoey. With the jammer in place, I knew I only had a maximum of two minutes to get it and get out before I could be tracked again. I walked across the room, knelt at my dresser, and removed the bottom drawer. Once I had pulled the drawer out and set it aside, I stuck my hand into the opening, popping the hidden compartment open. I pulled out the six-inch, cubed cardboard box. I cradled it gently, knowing that the item inside took up every bit of space in the small container.

I had been told what the item was and had heard stories about how important it was to Zoey's future, but I had never seen it myself. I took a moment to contemplate opening the box before I decided it would be better to wait. I stowed it away in my bag and put the drawer back in place. As I stood up and started to go, I heard a noise in the other room. It sounded like someone entering my room. Under different circumstances, I would have gone out and met whoever it was with my fists for breaking into my apartment. As it stood, Zoey's safety was more pressing.

I silently crossed my bedroom floor as the sounds of my home being trashed reached my ears. I slipped quietly into the closet, closing the door behind me. I could use the break-in noise to get back through the panel and lock it in place after me. At least I could be sure they wouldn't find us or the package I was delivering to Zoey. I could still hear them moving through the rooms, searching for something. This was the first time I had ever wished I had access to Race's spy cameras. I wanted to know who was ransacking my home and why.

But the mission was more important—I had to keep reminding myself that. Just keep to the task, and the rest will fall into place. At this point, I couldn't help but think about my "date" with Elena in her office a few days ago. I liked her and hated that it would seem as though I had just used her to get what I could and then took off. I had to trust that once this was all over, I would get a chance to explain the situation. Maybe she would forgive me, even if she never gave me a second chance. I knew going into this that my life would essentially be put on hold to protect Zoey. And up until now, I had never questioned that decision.

I would sacrifice myself to keep her safe. And I would do it with no regrets. I just couldn't stop that small part of me that wanted to move things forward with Elena from being jealous, impatient, and brooding. The sooner I could track down that book and get Zoey back on her quest, the sooner I would get my life back. I marched back to the hideout with purpose in my steps. I had no idea how I would return her memories, but I had a newfound determination to find a way.

Zoey was pouring over spell books and other texts when I walked in. She barely acknowledged my presence. "Anything good?" I tried to elicit a response from her, but she merely grunted at me and went back to her frantic note-taking and page-flipping. She seemed to be on to something, so the package would just have to wait a bit longer.

FORTY-FIVE

Zoey

JACK HAD COME BACK from who knew where and seemed like he wanted to talk. I just didn't have time for that. I had been researching for hours and thought I had come up with something that might help with my memories. There were articles about hypnosis and repressed memories, and if I paired that information with the meditation spells in one of these books, I just might be able to figure out what I needed to do.

If I was reading this right, I could perform the spell and then meditate, and somehow, it would lead me back to my forgotten memories. I just needed to gather some supplies and decide if I would tell Jack what I was doing. Given that I was a prisoner at the moment, I figured I would have to tell him. I knew he would worry, though, and it would just be easier if I could do the spell without him hovering. I couldn't decide if I wanted to tell him or not, so in the end, I opted to sleep on it first.

I read and re-read the spellbook and the hypnosis book until I was sure I had the passages memorized. It was late, and I could barely keep my eyes open. Jack had fallen asleep in the chair and looked miserable. I walked over and shook his shoulder. "Jack, come on, let's get some sleep. It's late."

As he started to stir, I realized there was only one bed down here. He looked at me, confused from just waking. "I'm sleeping here."

I shook my head adamantly. "No, you aren't. Come on. We might as well be family. I'm sure we can share a bed without crossing any lines." He started to argue with me, but I glared at him. "I said, come on. I meant it. Now, mister." And I walked away to get ready for bed. I had used that tone on Jack enough times that he knew I meant business. When I came out of the bathroom in my pajamas, he was already lying in bed, looking at me uneasily. "What?" I asked.

"I just don't want to mess this up, Zo. This mission is bigger than we are. And I'm not sure where you are with, well, everything. It's even more complicated since you don't remember the last six weeks."

"Jack, we aren't going to sleep together...OK, we are, but we're not having sex. Remember when we were kids, and it was perfectly acceptable for us to sleep in the same bed? That's what we're doing tonight. I'm not going to spoil your virtue for your lady love, don't worry." He seemed to relax at that, and I wondered who she was. "So, who is she? Now I'm curious." I winked at him as I sat down on the bed.

He looked at me with wide eyes, trying to look innocent. "I have no idea what you're talking about."

I punched him on the shoulder. "Liar. I know there's someone, or you wouldn't be acting so weird. Spill. Or else."

He winced at my minor threat. "OK, there might be someone, but I'm not even sure it's going to work out. This mission keeps getting in the way. Oh, I almost forgot!" He got up and ran off into the workshop.

I got up and followed him. It seemed like something substantial. "Jack, what did you forget? Where are you going?"

He appeared in the doorway before I could even make it out of the room. "This. It's a long story, and I can't tell you most of it, but you need this for your mission. This is the key." He handed me a six-inch cubed box made of cardboard.

"This box is the key?" I cocked an eyebrow at him.

He chuckled. "No, goofy, the key is inside. This is part of what the wizard had you chasing after. I was holding it until the time was right."

I studied the box in my hands. "And just what made you decide the time is right now?" He looked at his feet. "Oh, so that's one of the things you can't tell me? Jack, this is ridiculous. I can't complete a mission that I don't remember, and I can't help someone who won't talk to me. I'm done." I handed him the box and walked away.

He grabbed my arm before I could climb back into the bed. "Zoey, I'm sorry. I want to tell you everything, but I can't. I have a boss that I report to, and their identity can't be compromised right now. I've been given strict orders not to discuss who I'm working for and your protection. Please, don't walk away. Just open the box."

His pleading wore me down. I never could stay mad at him. "On one condition. You tell me everything you can about what's in this box and about my mission. You seem to know more than you should and way more than you let on at first. Also, where did you get that transporter in the other room?"

He nodded and chuckled. "I'll tell you what I can. I built the transporter. I got in a fair bit of trouble over it, too, with my boss. I broke a bunch of laws or something. Whatever. It saved your life—that's all I care about." He sat on the bed, placed the box between us, and motioned for me to sit as well. "I didn't come right out and admit it earlier, but I do work for a secret organization called the Resistance. They are in direct opposition to the Order, and they also work against the Planet Patrol on occasion. Some of the Resistance members are actually in the Patrol, and possibly the Order as well. I have proof that Race was working with the Order to steal the book from you. I know how that sounds, but he's the one who left me the proof. I loved him too. My boss stands to lose their position within the Patrol if it gets out that they are working with the Resistance. So, when it came out that the Patrol was looking for you, I was contracted to protect you, just as I had been when we were teens."

He paused and then pushed the box toward me. "All I know about your mission is that you need the item in this box, in addition to three other magical items, to help the wizard close the portal. Once the portal is closed, those who were born with magic will be the only ones who still have it."

I touched the box gingerly. "This item will help us do that? And that will stop the Order?" Jack nodded. "Then I guess I should see what it is." I picked up the box and gently peeled back the tape that sealed it closed. I looked at Jack expectantly and then opened the flaps of the box. Inside was a twelve-sided die, a dodecahedron, that appeared to be made of copper. It was shimmering as though it was alive. "It's beautiful. Can I touch it?" Jack looked concerned but shrugged his shoulders. I guessed they hadn't told him if it was OK to handle the item— just that he had to keep it safe for me. I couldn't help but wonder who this wizard was and what he had asked me to do for him.

I gently turned the dodecahedron out of the box into my hand. It was warm to the touch, with a slowly pulsing glow about it. It may have been the most beautiful thing I had ever seen. The moment I touched it, I could feel the power flow through me. It was unlike anything I had ever experienced. I felt as though I had been asleep my entire life, and for the first time, I was awake. My senses seemed to be heightened. Sounds were louder; colors were brighter...everything seemed sharper, somehow. I wondered if there was a way for this thing to help me regain my memories. I hadn't found any texts about it, though, so I had nothing to go on except for instinct. My instincts called me to the glowing orb, as though we were two parts to a whole and belonged together. "How does it work?" I asked Jack, knowing that he would have no idea.

"I've never even seen that thing until just now. I have no clue how to make it work. I was always told that you would know what to do."

I nodded my head. Maybe if I meditated, the answer would come to me. I gently placed the polyhedron into the box and closed it back the way it had been. The package looked as though it had never been opened. "We need to put this somewhere safe until we can figure out where the book is and get to it." I handed the box back to Jack. I didn't even have my backpack, so I had no place to stash the thing. Jack walked over to the wall, hit a panel, and opened a secret compartment. Once the box was safely inside, he closed the door and walked back to the bed. I couldn't even tell where the panel was. So, I was sure the dodecahedron would be safe.

I woke suddenly to noise on Jack's side of the bed. I felt weird like my brain was foggy. I tried to sit up but I couldn't. I turned my head to the right, opening my eyes to see another familiar face besides Jack.

"Elena? What are you doing here? What's going on?" My words sounded slurred to me, and my tongue felt thick. I watched as she jabbed a syringe into Jack's arm, pushing the plunger down to release whatever she was injecting. It was as though she didn't hear what I had said. Then she turned her back on us and pulled out her comm device.

"I have them drugged and bound, and I have the package. We're ready for extraction." She held the small cubed box up as she spoke, and the darkness took me under.

The Story Continues...

Don't miss out on the rest of the story!
  Check out the next book:

Betrayed: Forged by Magic – Book 2

Kidnapped twice in one week? My life is out of control.

Just as I'm getting over the shock of being transported back to Calliope, causing me to lose my memories of the past six weeks, I'm drugged and taken by someone I thought I could trust.

My best friend Jack says I'm supposed to save the world, but I have no idea what he's talking about. My mind is a fragmented mess:

A wizard with a magic book
A bunch of artifacts I have to track down
A strange creature made of smoke
A pair of amber eyes that haunt my dreams
A name...Kyro

If only I could figure out how those pieces fit together, maybe I could get back what I've lost.

I have to figure out who I can trust and fast. It sounds like the Patrol is closing in on me, and the Order isn't far behind.

Since I found out that Jack has been hiding things from me for years, I feel completely alone. I have to find a way to get my memories back if I'm going to complete this mission.

Making my way back to the Sea Shadow proves more difficult than anticipated. I'm desperate to get back to the quest. Is it because of what's at stake or the feelings of passion when I dream of Kyro?

The world is counting on me, and I'm running out of time.

Click below to get Betrayed:

https://books2read.com/forgedbymagic-betrayed

About the Author

M.P. Starkweather is a wife, mother, author, poet, casual online gamer, self-proclaimed fan-girl, and full-time nerd. She writes free-form poetry, paranormal romance, sci-fi romance, reverse harem romance, omegaverse romance, and is branching out into contemporary romance. In her free time, she enjoys writing, reading, Dungeons & Dragons, table top games with her husband and friends, and playing with her son. M.P. also enjoys tv, movies, and music across various genres.

To get the most up-to-date information about her latest releases and book signings, check out www.mpstarkweather.

com or follow her on your favorite social media site.

Also By M.P. Starkweather

<u>Christmas or Knot</u>
Standalones – Paranormal RH

<u>The Wayward Girl</u>
The Cursed Blade Series – Paranormal w/ different pairings

<u>Digital Blade</u> – RH
Elemental Blade – RH
Vampires at Midnight - Paranormal RH series
<u>Blood Moon</u>

<u>Blood Lost</u>

<u>Blood War</u>

<u>Vampires at Midnight: The Complete Trilogy</u>
VaM/HoF Crossover Novella - Paranormal RH

<u>Blood Wolf</u>— free with newsletter signup
Hunters of the Forest - Paranormal RH series

<u>Wolf Bane</u>

<u>Wolf Caged</u>

<u>Wolf Moon</u>

<u>Hunters of the Forest: The Complete Trilogy</u>
Forged by Magic - Sci-fi/Fantasy M/F series

<u>Hidden</u>

<u>Betrayed</u>

<u>Saved</u>

<u>Forged by Magic: The Complete Trilogy</u>
Daydreams and Sunsets - a collection of poetry

<u>Daydreams and Sunsets</u>